THE BABY
PROJECT

THE BABY PROJECT

BY

GRACE GREEN

MILLS & BOON®

*All the characters in t... ...istence outside
the imagination of t... ...author, and have no relation
whatsoever to anyone ...
They are not even dis...
known or unknown to ...author, and all the incidents
are ...*

*All Rights Reserved inciuuing the right of reproduction
in whole or in part in any form. This edition is published
by arrangement with Harlequin Enterprises II B.V. The
text of this publication or any part thereof may not be
reproduced or transmitted in any form or by any means,
electronic or mechanical, including photocopying,
recording, storage in an information retrieval system,
or otherwise, without the written permission of
the publisher.*

*First published in Great Britain 2000
Large Print edition 2000
Harlequin Mills & Boon Limited,
Eton House, 18-24 Paradise Road,
Richmond, Surrey TW9 1SR*

ISBN 0 263 16728 3

*Set in Times Roman 16½ on 18 pt.
16-1200-47439*

*Printed and bound in Great Britain
by Antony Rowe Ltd, Chippenham, Wiltshire*

CHAPTER ONE

"JORDAN CAINE is a cad!"

"Oh, he is, Angelina!" Outrage sparked in Monique's faded blue eyes. "Leaving our dear sweet Mallory to cope on her own all these months without so much as a postcard."

"Well, the man does appear to be an *adventurer*." Eighty-year-old Emily looked anxiously at the other two over her half glasses. "But sisters, we've never even met Mr. Caine. Shouldn't we give him the benefit of the doubt?"

Angelina sighed. "Emily, you can be very trying. Any man who has behaved as badly as he has doesn't deserve—"

The front doorbell chimed, making them all start. They looked at each other meaningfully, and then with one accord set their bedtime mugs of hot milk on the coffee table.

"She's here," whispered Emily. "Let us have no more talk of Jordan Caine."

All three cocked their heads and listened.

From their cosy nook in the sitting room, they heard brisk footsteps cross the hall. Then they heard the front door opening and Elsa, their landlady, say warmly, "Mallory, come away in. How was your trip? It's almost midnight! I was beginning to worry about you."

"I'm so sorry, Elsa. My last day of work, and so many loose ends to tidy…and then the staff surprised me with a Goodbye party and there was no way I could disappoint…"

The voices faded.

After several minutes, during which time the sisters sat tensely without talking, they heard steps approaching. Catching their breath, they turned towards the door and waited.

The door opened.

When Mallory appeared in the doorway, they sighed with pleasure at the sight of her. She looked lovely as always, in a short-skirted black suit, with an ivory shirt and stylish black pumps. Her face was pale and her features strained, but her genuine smile brought her dusky brown eyes to life.

"Hi, ladies," she said. "Isn't it past your bedtime?"

Not for the world would they have told her they had waited up to make sure she arrived safely.

"Just finishing our hot milk," Angelina murmured.

"I'm going along to Number Five now." Mallory raised both hands and shoved back her unruly auburn locks. "But I hope you'll drop by and visit tomorrow."

"Everything's settled?" Monique asked.

"Everything's settled."

"So," Emily's tone was awed, "you've burned your boats."

"Burned my boats and my bridges and everything else." Mallory's wry smile brought a dimple to her right cheek. "From now on, the only way to go is forward."

"Good luck, dear," they chorused.

"Thank you. I'm going to need it!"

With a little wave, she closed the door and walked back into the hallway.

Elsa was waiting for her, with the baby in her arms.

"He's teething," Elsa said as she carefully handed over the infant. "He was cranky earlier, but he's settled now."

Mallory felt her heart melt with love as she looked down at the sleeping child. Tenderly she ran a finger over his flushed cheeks. "Poor mite."

"I was along at Number Five earlier and aired out all the bedding. Just pop him in his crib and with a bit of luck he'll sleep through till morning."

"I hope so." Mallory stifled a huge yawn. "I'll be out like a light myself as soon as my head hits the pillow."

Jordan Caine slammed the door of his scarlet Lexus, slung his leather travel bag over his shoulder, and strode purposefully up the drive to Number Five Seaside Lane.

The rambling old house was beautifully silvered by moonlight, but he paid little attention to it or any of his other surroundings. This place didn't interest him. If there was one thing he hated, it was small-town living. He planned to sleep in the house tonight; put it on the market tomorrow; and be on his way again by lunchtime…shaking the beach sand of this sea-salty little Washington resort from his size eleven boots before it had time to stick.

Sliding his key into the lock, he opened the front door and stepped inside. Moonlight streamed down through the skylight above the staircase, and in its bone-white wash, he saw that the roomy hallway was very sparsely furnished.

The only other time he'd been in this house it had been empty. As he'd discussed terms with the Seashore realtor, his voice had echoed back from the bare walls. Apart from a few sticks of furniture the house seemed just as empty now—

A creaking sound came from his left. He spun around as sharply as if it had been a gunshot.

Then frustrated by his hair-trigger reaction, he swore. He hadn't realized his nerves were still so badly on edge….

The sound had come from the downstairs bedroom. He crossed the hall, turned the doorknob with a stealthy hand, and warily pushed the door inwards.

A low-wattage bedside lamp cast a pool of light over the empty bed, leaving most of the room in shadow—

His heart gave an erratic lurch when he saw that someone—a woman—was slumped in a rocking chair by the bed.

She was asleep; he could hear her regular breathing.

Her face was in shadow but he could see that she had a luxuriant tumble of long curly hair. She was wearing a light shirt with a dark suit; the jacket lay untidily open, the skirt had ridden halfway up her thighs. Her legs—long fantastic legs—were stretched out before her and a pair of high-heeled pumps lay askew on the carpet.

She shifted position and her head lolled sideways, towards the light, giving him a clear view of her face.

His first thought was: "Wow, what a stunner!"

His second thought was a shocked and furious: *"It's that Madison woman!"*

What the hell was *she* doing here? Clenching his hands into fists, he glared at her. He felt an overwhelming urge to grab her by the shoulders, shake her from her sleep, and demand that she explain what she was doing in his house.

His scowl deepened as his gaze flicked to the framed photograph sitting on the bedside table. He recognized it as one of the pictures taken on his sister's wedding day.

Even as grief tore at him afresh, he felt the old anger rise to block it out. He wanted to smash the picture against the wall—the picture of his sister Janine and that man, looking besottedly at each other. To their right, Mallory Madison, maid of honour, her eyes bright with joy. To their left, Jordan Caine, best man, his happy expression an utter travesty. He'd put on an Oscar-calibre performance that day, in order not to spoil his sister's wedding.

A wedding that would never have taken place if Mallory Madison hadn't given the couple her full support, over his own strenuous objections to the marriage.

For that, he would never forgive her.

But it would be a huge mistake to waken her now and confront her—after his recent harrowing ordeal, his emotions were far too volatile. Better to wait till he'd had a good night's sleep and was more in control of himself.

After giving her one last black glower, he left the room and made his way wearily up the stairs.

There were four bedrooms on this level, and when he opened the door to the first, he found it was furnished with a single bed and a small dresser. The room was obviously not currently in use—it was bare of personal items and the air was stale. He would make it his. Just for the night.

Tossing down his travel bag, he crossed impatiently to the window and pushed it open. Outside, moonlight spangled the jet-black ocean; stars winked down from an indigo sky. And summer scents swept in on the ocean breeze, invoking a poignancy that caught him unawares and made his throat ache.

Irritably, he tugged the curtains shut. And turning away, he crossed to the bed. Stripping to his jeans, he crashed on top of the covers. And within seconds, he was fast asleep.

Mallory awoke at dawn.

And she realized, to her dismay, that she had fallen asleep in the rocking chair, where she'd sat down for a moment after she'd settled Matthew in his crib. She must have been even more exhausted than she'd thought!

Getting up, she stretched to iron out the kinks in her muscles, and then, with an anticipatory smile, she tiptoed over to the crib in the far corner of the room.

Matthew was still asleep. And as always, her heart turned to mush when she looked at the nine-month-old baby. She couldn't have loved him more if he'd been her own...

And once Jordan Caine had relinquished any claim to the child—as he undoubtedly would, since he'd shown no interest in him till this date—she could legally *make* him her own.

The problem was she hadn't the faintest idea where the man was—all her efforts to contact him had been in vain. She hadn't spoken to him for months—not since the day his sister and Tom had died in a train crash and she'd called to tell him. She knew, of course, how he felt about Tom but she'd believed he truly cared for Janine and she found it *unforgivable* that he hadn't come home for her funeral.

The thought lingered sourly as she padded through to the kitchen and put on a pot of coffee. But as she looked around the big homey room and pictured her new life at Number Five with Matthew, her spirits rose again.

Humming under her breath, she slipped off her rumpled suit jacket and slung it over the back of Matthew's high chair. While she waited for the coffee to drip, she cut two slices of whole-wheat bread and popped them in the toaster.

Still humming, she pulled back the yellow-and-white gingham curtains. But as she did, two things impinged on her senses and froze the breath in her throat:

She saw a racy scarlet Lexus sitting in the drive…

And she heard a floorboard squeak behind her.

She whirled around. And shock slammed through her when she saw a dark-bearded stranger looming in the kitchen doorway. His hair was black and shaggy; his hands were fisted; and his gray eyes were fixed on her with a ferocious intensity that could only mean murder.

She lunged for the bread knife and clutching the handle with both hands, held it out in front of her, the tip of the razor-sharp blade pointed directly at him.

"I don't know who you are," she said in a shrill voice. "And I don't know what you want, but get out! Right now!"

The stranger raised a cynical eyebrow. "Why, Mallory, dear!" Sarcasm reverberated in his husky baritone voice. "Is that any way to greet your brother-in-law?"

"Brother-in-law?" The knife trembled in her fingers. "What are you talking about? I don't have a—"

"Strictly speaking, no. But since your brother was married to my sister, I guess that's the closest I can come to describing our... relationship."

Mallory struggled to catch her breath. She gawked disbelievingly, trying to verify his claim, trying to recognize the man behind the black stubbled beard.

She'd met Janine's brother only once, on the day of the wedding, but then he'd been clean-shaven and elegant and—she'd had to admit it—devastatingly attractive in a black tux. He'd looked like a movie star. This man was scruffy and edgy and wearing nothing but an old pair of blue jeans. He looked like a prisoner on the run.

The man she remembered had been tall and solidly built. This man was tall, but he didn't have a spare ounce of flesh on his darkly tanned body. He was lean and hard and—

"Oh, it's me," he drawled. "Or are you staring because you get your jollies out of looking at a man's half-naked torso?"

She wrenched her gaze from his powerfully muscled chest and opened her mouth to let fly with a scathing retort, only to have the angry words dry up in her throat. He'd raked back his hair, revealing an inch-long white scar on his forehead. A scar she recognized.

This was indeed Jordan Caine. As she assimilated the fact, she felt faint with relief. For months she'd tried desperately to get in touch with this man so she could put her plans in motion. Now—oh, joy!—he was here.

Controlling a rush of euphoria, she set the knife on the counter. "How did you get into the house?"

"I have a key. Which was just as well—I doubt you'd have heard me if I'd rung the bell, you were out like a light. By the way, you'll be glad to know you don't snore."

She stared at him. ''What? How do you know—''

''I arrived in the early hours but before I went upstairs I heard a movement in that bedroom so I checked it out. You were sound asleep in a creaky old rocking chair.''

''You mean...you *slept* here?''

''Of course.''

Her mind boggled at the absolute gall of the man—walking into the house like that, as if he owned it! With an effort, she held onto her temper. ''What do you want?''

''Right now,'' he said with a mocking smile, ''what I want is coffee. Did you happen to make enough for—''

The toast popped up and to her astonishment, he whirled towards the sound, his body taut. The spring-loaded reaction made her blink. She'd sensed the man was on edge but this was ridiculous. Curiosity burned inside her—

But when he turned to her again, his eyes had a diamond-hard glitter. A warning glitter. *Mind your own business.* He didn't say the words; he didn't need to.

She swallowed back her half-formed questions. "I didn't make enough coffee for two, but help yourself. I'll put on another pot when I've had my shower."

"And we'll talk. You have a bit of explaining to do."

"*I* have a bit of explaining to do?" She glowered at him. "You've got to be kidding! You're the one who—"

"Could you pass me a mug?"

Lips compressed, she reached into the cupboard. He stepped over and held out his hand. As he took the mug, she caught a hint of his musky male scent. It was earthy as a dark forest, erotic as an intimate caress. She felt an unfamiliar tingling sensation deep down inside her...a sensation that was as unsettling as it was unwelcome.

She drew back sharply, but not before she'd seen his mouth slant in a knowing smile.

"I guess," he murmured maliciously as he poured his coffee, "you're not used to having a half-naked male around in the morning. Sorry if I'm disturbing you—"

"On the contrary," she retorted with a haughty tilt of her chin, "I'm quite used to having a half-naked male around in the morning—and not only in the kitchen, but in my bed!''

She whirled away from him and stalked out of the kitchen, her cheeks burning. But even as she hurried to the bedroom, she heard his mocking laughter follow her.

The sooner she got rid of him the better, she decided angrily—though she must be careful not to antagonize him. He could so easily put obstacles in the way of her becoming Matthew's legal guardian, and that was to be avoided at all costs. No, on the surface she'd have to be nice to Jordan Caine. It would be a very small price to pay in the end.

She closed the bedroom door and tiptoed over to check on Matthew. He was still asleep, thank goodness. She hoped he wouldn't waken till after she and his uncle had had their talk. She didn't want to be distracted during what was going to be the most important conversation of her life.

''Right, let's have that talk.'' Jordan leaned back against the countertop, watching Ms. Madison through narrowed eyes as she made a fresh pot of coffee. Earlier, tousle-haired and terrified, with yesterday's lipstick and mascara smudged—and with a scalpel-sharp bread knife pointed directly at his heart!—she'd looked sexy as hell. Now, in a demure green T-shirt and perky shorts, with her hair neatly scooped up in a topknot and her face scrubbed clean, she looked even sexier. Too bad she was a redhead; the situation could have been interesting. "For starters, what are you doing here?"

"That's exactly what I was going to ask you." Taking toast from the toaster, she crossed to the table. "But okay, I'll go first. I've moved in. As of last night."

He did a double take. "Moved in?"

She buttered the toast. "I plan on living here." She reached for the marmalade. "For the foreseeable future."

"In this house? Are we talking about the same place? Number Five Seaside Lane?"

She turned to him, her brown eyes faintly surprised. "Yes. Do you have a problem with that?"

He paused for a moment, and then faking an encouraging tone that set his teeth on edge, he said, "Tell me more about these plans of yours. As I recall, you had a job in Seattle…?"

His nonthreatening manner had its desired effect; he could see her relax, could see he'd put her off-guard.

"That's right," she said. And added impulsively, "I have to admit that the last several months haven't been easy. I've driven here every Friday after work, gone back to Seattle every Sunday night. It's been *awful,* not being with Matthew through the week. I've missed him so much—but now we can be together all the time and I'm so happy about that. You'll get to meet him in a minute," she added with a smile. "He's still asleep, but he should be wakening soon."

She'd brought a lover here? Jordan stared at her incredulously. "He slept in this house last night?"

"Mmm."

"He wasn't in your bed!"

"I don't let him into my bed every night— only when he's whiny."

"*Whiny?*" Good grief, what kind of a wimp *was* the guy!

''Look, I'm not expecting you to get involved with him. In fact, I'm assuming you won't want to and I'd actually prefer that you didn't. But it would be nice if you could send him a postcard once in a while when you're abroad—''

''Are you out of your *mind?* I want nothing to do with him. I don't even want to see him!''

His vehemence obviously jolted her; but at the same time he saw an expression of relief in her eyes.

''Then that will make everything easier for me,'' she said. ''I was afraid that if you once held him in your arms you might fall in love with him and want him for yourself.''

''What the *hell* do you—''

''I'm sorry, but try to see it from my point of view. I've been trying to contact you for months so we could straighten everything out but when I didn't hear from you, I decided to forge on with my own plans on the assumption that you wanted nothing to do with the situation. You can't blame me, since you didn't even bother to come home for the funeral! And since you told me at the wedding that you'd never forgive me for supporting Tom and

Janine when they wanted to marry, I figured I'd never see you again.''

''My sister was barely eighteen,'' he snapped. ''Your brother got her pregnant when she was little more than a child herself. He was twenty-four, and took advantage of a girl who was immature and—''

''They married because they were in love.''

''There's no point in discussing this now. It's water under the bridge. But you're right about one thing. I'll never forgive you for the part you played—''

''I don't want your forgiveness. Nor do I need it. As for Tom, you never *did* understand him. You didn't take the time to get to know him and if you had, you'd have learned what a fine and decent man he was.''

''No decent man would have—'' He sliced his hand down in a dismissive gesture. ''We're only rehashing what we said on their wedding day. Let's get back on track. Tell me about these plans of yours…to live in this house.''

Before answering, she poured her coffee and set the yellow ceramic mug on the table. When she spoke, it was quietly.

"Tom and Janine had signed the lease for a year and on their death it still had several months to run so I took over the payments. The lease came up for renewal last month and I signed the contract for another year at the same rate." She toyed abstractedly with her thin gold necklace. "It's a beautiful house, I can't imagine why the owner lets it out so cheaply. I asked the woman at the Realty Management company but she didn't know. All she could tell me was that the arrangements had been made through the owner's lawyer."

"Well, that all sounds fine and dandy." Jordan's lips thinned. "But 'there's many a slip 'twixt the cup and the lip'! And I see one little obstacle in your way."

A frown crinkled her creamy skin into a neat little V between her eyebrows. "What do you mean?"

"Sit down," he said, "and drink your coffee before it gets cold. I'm going up to have my shower. When I come back down again...I have something to tell you."

Mallory stared after him as he left the kitchen. What on earth did he mean: an obstacle? It had sounded ominous, yet she had everything under control…didn't she? The house was hers for at least the next eleven months, and Matthew would be hers forever—his uncle had made it more than plain that he had no interest in the child.

She sat down and drank her coffee. She usually loved that first kick of it the morning, but today it had no effect.

She couldn't shake a dreadful feeling of foreboding.

She was still trying, without success, to figure out what Jordan Caine could possibly be going to tell her, when she heard the sound of a vehicle chugging up the drive.

Getting up, she looked out the window, over the garden fence, and saw a truck parking behind the Lexus. On the panel, it said AB Movers, the company she'd hired to cart her belongings from Seattle.

Well, at least, she reflected dryly as she hurried to open the front door, *something* was going according to plan!

CHAPTER TWO

JORDAN HALTED abruptly on the landing.
When he'd come upstairs earlier, the front hall
had been empty except for a D-shaped phone
table and a spindly chair beside it. Now it was
crammed with boxes and furniture and all sorts
of other paraphernalia…and in the midst of the
chaos stood Mallory.

''What the *devil's* going on?'' he called
down.

She looked up. ''My things have arrived
from Seattle.''

Her *things?* Dammit, this was an added
complication and one he didn't need. He
fought to contain his intense frustration as he
glowered at the cardboard boxes…and the several bookcases, the chairs, the pine desk…an
oil painting, a dozen potted plants, a set of
wicker furniture—

Two men in beige overalls appeared in the
doorway, their name tags proclaiming them to

be Archie and Rock. Archie and Rock were carrying a teal-blue sofa.

"Where do you want this, miss?" asked Archie.

"In there, please." Mallory indicated the sitting room, to her right.

As the men hefted the sofa into the room, Jordan pounded down the stairs.

"Mallory—"

She turned to him, and he saw that her cheeks were flushed, her forehead moist. "I know you want to talk to me." She shoved back a clump of auburn hair that had tumbled from her topknot. "But it'll have to wait till the men have finished—"

"Get rid of it."

"I beg your pardon?"

He waved a hand around the hall. "This stuff can't stay here. Tell the men to take it away."

She looked at him as if he were speaking in tongues. "Would you please go through to the kitchen while I see to this?" Rolling her eyes, she turned her back on him. "Whatever it is you want to talk about will have to wait."

He grasped her shoulders and spun her around again. "This *is* what I want to talk about. You can't stay here. Tell these men to take your things and pack them back in their truck and—"

"Sorry, mister, no can do." Rock and Archie had come out of the sitting room. Rock handed Mallory a triplicated form. "You've checked the number of pieces?"

She nodded.

"Then sign here and we'll be on our way."

Impatiently, Jordan said, "I'm telling you, Mallory, I don't want you living here any more. You can't—"

Ignoring him, she signed the form.

As Rock ripped off her copy and gave it to her, he grinned at Jordan. "Don't want her to move back in, buddy? You're making a big mistake." He ran an appreciative gaze over Mallory and winked. "This one's a keeper, mate!"

Sidestepping the boxes, the two men left, leaving the front door wide open behind them.

Jordan looked exasperatedly at Mallory. "You're going to have to get this stuff out of here—"

"And you're beginning to sound like a broken record." Anger made her eyes tawny as a tiger's. "I told you, I've rented this house for the next year and—" She broke off with a "Tsk!" as a rattling noise came from her bedroom.

"That's Matthew," she said. "He's awake—and no wonder, with all the fuss you've been making!" She brushed past him. "But you may as well come and meet him now. He's at his best, first thing in the morning."

"I've told you," Jordan said grimly, "I don't *want* to meet him. What I want is for the two of you to get out of this house right away—"

But she had disappeared into the bedroom.

And next thing, he heard her say in a tender voice, "So you're awake, are you, sweetheart?" A chuckle. Then, "Oh, Matthew, get your fingers out of my hair…!" A second's silence, followed by the unmistakable sound of a kiss.

He needed this situation like he needed a hole in his head! Gritting his teeth, Jordan rounded a wicker chair— cursing as he tripped over a vacuum cleaner—and stormed out through the front door. Then with resentment exuding from every pore, he strode down the drive, across the deserted street, and over the salt grass to the beach.

Three miles to the south jutted a rugged cape, with an inn nestled in its sheltering embrace. To the north, the small town followed the curve of the beach to a marina, where he could see yachts bobbing alongside narrow jetties.

He paused for a second, and then headed north.

The realtor's office was on the town's main street. He'd walk there now and list the house. That way, when he talked with Ms. Madison again, it would be a fait accompli. The moment the place sold, her lease would automatically be nullified. And it should sell fast, because he would ask a reasonable price. He didn't need the money. What he needed was to get that woman out of his life, once and for all.

''He's been gone a couple of hours, Elsa.'' Mallory grimaced as she glanced out the sitting room window. ''But I can see him coming back now—along the beach. Don't forget to tell the sisters not to come around today. I'll give them a call when things settle down.''

''Why has he come to Seashore?'' Elsa's voice came worriedly over the phone line. ''He never visited while Janine was alive. Do you think he wants Matthew?''

''Oh, no. He's made it plain he wants nothing to do with him.''

''Well, *that's* good!''

''Mmm.'' Mallory rubbed a hand over her nape. ''But I feel uneasy. He's been acting so strangely. Why would he think he had the right to order me to send my stuff back?''

''In my humble opinion, the man's a control freak. Look how he tried to run Janine's life! Now she's gone, he wants to run yours too. But I recall Janine saying her brother hated small towns, so I don't imagine he'll hang around.''

Mallory's nerves tightened as she watched Jordan cross the street, his lean energetic frame set off to perfection in a white T-shirt and taupe shorts. His beard gave him a rakish appearance and as she took in his black hair and rugged features, she had to admit he was an eye-catching sight. But he certainly was not her type! She liked men who were kind and compassionate; strong yet tender—

"Mallory?" Elsa's voice broke into her musings. "Are you still there?"

"Mm? Oh...yes, Elsa, but I have to go now."

"Good luck, dear. Let me know what happens."

Mallory put down the phone and turning from the window, she scooped up Matthew, who was on his stomach, worming his way over the carpet. Slipping his blue T-shirt into his pants, she tucked him into the crook of one arm.

"You're the most beautiful baby in the world." She kissed his brow and inhaled the sweet scent of his skin. "And I want you to be a good boy when you meet your uncle. I know he doesn't want to see you, but it wouldn't be right to let him leave town without at least saying hello. He's a bit of an ogre. Do you think you're up to it?"

"Goo," he gurgled. And tried to reach her topknot.

She laughed softly and arched her head back. "Oh, you just love to get your fingers into my hair, don't you!" As she spoke, she heard steps crunching up the drive. And her pulse quickened when she heard Jordan come into the house.

"Mallory!" His deep voice reverberated from the front hall. The voice of a drill sergeant! "Where are you?"

With a fingertip, she tidied a wisp of Matthew's hair. "Okay, sweetie," she whispered, "let's get this over with."

Bracing herself, she walked out to the hall. Jordan Caine was standing amid her belongings, with his back to her.

"I'm here," she said.

As he turned, he held out a long white envelope. "I want you to read this—" He broke off when he saw the baby, and his brow lowered in a dark frown. "What's going on?"

"I know you don't want anything to do with Matthew, but it's not going to kill you to say hi!"

Jordan stared at the baby wriggling in her arms, the infant's gaze glued to her topknot as he endeavoured to reach it. *This* was Matthew?

Well, he'd really screwed up there, hadn't he! But it surprised him to see the delectable Ms. Madison with a child. She certainly hadn't looked pregnant at her brother's wedding...

He recalled Janine telling him that Tom's sister was thirty-one and single. And he recalled saying irately to Janine, when she told him that unlike him, Mallory was enthusiastic about the upcoming marriage, "Tell that dried-up old spinster to butt out of our lives!"

That was before he'd met her, of course, and when he did meet her, on the wedding day, he'd found out that far from being dried-up, she was lush as a ripe exotic fruit. But not, definitely not, his type. He felt about redheads the way he felt about small towns...and about babies!

"I know this must be upsetting for you." Mallory's voice was apologetic. "I'm sorry. And I know how against the marriage you were, but Janine loved you so much, and I know she'd have wanted you to love this baby too."

"Why the heck would Janine care if I loved this kid or not? Look, read my lips. I don't like babies. And I have no interest in this one or any other. So if you'll just put him back in his crib or whatever, then you and I can get on with business. This—'' he waggled the white envelope at her ''—is a contract I've just signed with Burton Barton, the local realtor. I've put the house up for sale.''

''House? Which house?''

''This house.''

''*This* house?''

''Number Five Seaside Lane. It's mine.''

She couldn't have looked more stunned if he'd told her he'd planted a bomb in the basement. ''It *can't* be yours!''

He felt a pang of compunction when he saw the panic in her eyes. He ignored it. ''I bought it before the wedding, when I knew you'd beaten me and that come hell or high water those two were going to tie the knot—''

''It wasn't a case of beating you! It wasn't a competition, to see who would win—I just wanted what was best for Tom and Janine—''

''All the arrangements were made through my lawyer,'' he continued tersely. ''I knew your brother had taken a job in Seashore and I knew they were having a hard time finding a rental place they could afford so I bought this house and made sure they learned it was available—and for a minimal rent, because I wanted my sister to live comfortably.''

''Did *they* know,'' she asked, ''that it was yours?''

''No.''

''You did that for them?'' This secret, generous gesture put him in a new light. Mallory felt herself soften towards him. ''That was so kind of you—''

''I did it for Janine,'' he interrupted rudely. ''I no longer have any need of the place. End of story.''

Her momentary softness dissipated in a flash. ''I've signed a one-year lease,'' she said in a defiant tone. ''So you can't evict me. At least, not till the year is up.''

''I can,'' he said. ''And I intend to. The moment the property changes hands, your lease becomes null and void.''

She seemed to shrink back from him. Then she shook her head and her upper lip curled. Unmistakably, contemptuously curled. ''You're quite something, Jordan Caine.''

He hadn't known that tawny brown eyes could look so cold. ''It's business,'' he said curtly. "And there's no room for sentiment in business."

"Tom was wrong about you. He believed that despite your overbearing attitude, you were a good man at heart. I'm glad he's not here to see that you have no heart at all." She clenched her jaw as she prepared to humble herself. "Can you at least let me keep the house for the summer, to give me time to look for someplace else?"

"No can do. It's May already and Barton's going to advertise Number Five as an ideal house for a bed-and-breakfast business, so it will be to a buyer's advantage to move in immediately, before the start of the tourist season."

"You'd throw me out in the street—with this baby?" She took in a deep breath and when she went on, her voice had a distinct tremor in it. "I gave up my job in Seattle so that I could work at home and be a good mother to Matthew. I'm on a very tight budget now. I'd never have been able to swing it if I hadn't been able to factor in the low rent."

"That's not *my* problem. Before you got yourself pregnant, you should have looked to

the future. Where's the baby's father? Doesn't
he contribute to his upkeep?''

She gaped at him as if he'd sprouted an extra head.

He stabbed the envelope at her. ''It's your
responsibility and his. Not mine. What happened anyway? Did he dump you, or did—''

''You think—'' she swallowed hard ''—that
this is *my* baby?''

He raised a cynical eyebrow. ''If he isn't,''
he retorted, ''then whose is he?''

''He's Janine's, of course!'' She sounded as
if she was spelling out something incredibly
simple to a dim-witted child.

''You're lying.'' He glared at her. ''Janine
died in the train wreck.'' He felt an ache in his
heart, the same ache he always felt when he
thought about his sister. ''She was eight
months pregnant, but—''

''Janine had her baby two weeks before the
accident!''

He stared at her, his mind reeling.

Hugging Matthew close, she went on in a
tone of utter dismay, ''Didn't she call you at
the time and let you know?''

He felt the hair at his nape prickle. "You're saying...this is really Janine's child?"

She nodded. "Yes, this is really her child."

"Dear God." He exhaled a shaky breath. "No, Janine didn't call...our arrangement was that I would phone *her*. I knew I'd be out in the jungle most of the time so I told her I'd be incommunicado in August but I'd get back to the mining camp around her due date and give her a call. I was actually back earlier than I'd expected, but before I had a chance to call her, you phoned with the news about the train crash. I was *shattered* when you told me Janine and Tom had died—and when I asked about the baby, you said there were no survivors in that compartment of the train. I assumed Janine was still pregnant, of course. And at that point, you broke down so I didn't press you for details."

"I'd told you everything I knew. But...didn't you get the message I left for you at the camp the following day?"

"No." He frowned. "I didn't get any message."

"Jordan, the police turned up at my apartment, hours after they'd notified me about

Tom and Janine. They told me the baby had been found in the wreckage, miraculously alive and unhurt. I phoned the camp a second time but you weren't there so I left a message.'' Tears welled up and she blinked them back. ''I can't believe you didn't get it.''

He struggled to get his thoughts in order. ''Why were Janine and Tom traveling by train with a new baby?''

''They were on their way home from L.A.— they'd gone down there for a friend's wedding. Matthew was born there.''

''Was he premature?''

''No, he was a full-term baby—Janine had made a mistake with her dates. Anyway, Matthew decided during the wedding reception that he was ready to make his way into the world! After they got him out of hospital, Tom and Janine stayed on in their friends' apartment for ten days. Then they bought a car seat to transport Matthew home.'' Mallory's voice trembled. ''The police said it saved his little life.''

For a long moment, she and Jordan looked at each other in silence. Without taking her eyes from him, she wiped a tear away with a fingertip. And then another.

"So," she whispered finally, "where do we go from here?"

"Janine's baby. It's...hard to take this in."

She smiled wanly through her tears. "He looks like Janine, except for the fair hair." As she spoke, she moved over to him. "Isn't he adorable?"

Dazedly, he looked at the infant but as soon as Matthew saw him, the child emitted a scream of terror.

"Honey!" Mallory's tone was startled. "What's wrong?"

The baby wrenched himself around and grabbing her shirt, buried his face against her bosom. But even that didn't altogether muffle his screams.

"Sweetie, what's the matter?" asked Mallory urgently. "What *is* it?"

The child twisted his head around, eyes flooded with tears, but the mere sight of Jordan sent him off into a renewed session of frantic screaming.

"It would seem," Jordan said in an ironic tone, "that my nephew doesn't like me."

"Hush, Matthew, hush, sweetheart." Mallory held the baby against her shoulder and rubbed his back soothingly. To Jordan, she said, "It must be your beard."

"He's never seen a beard before?"

"He's not used to men—bearded *or* clean-shaven. Through the week, Elsa has been looking after him—"

"Elsa?"

"Elsa Carradine. She lives a few doors along from here. She's been baby-sitting Matthew during the week. Matthew's used to being with her, and with her boarders—the three Barnley sisters."

The baby's screams had been replaced by convulsive sobs. Mallory went on hurriedly, "I'm going to take him through to the bedroom and settle him, then I'll put him down for his nap. When I come back, we'll talk."

She added, as she left, "And I hope you'll rethink your decision to sell the house, now that you know the reason for my present financial situation."

Worn out after his crying bout, Matthew fell asleep as soon as Mallory tucked him into his crib.

Glad to have a quiet moment to herself, she crossed to the bedroom window and looked out. What a shock it had been to discover that Jordan owned the house—and that he was the one who had set the incredibly low rent. She could hardly believe he'd behaved so generously, considering how adamantly he'd opposed the marriage.

How the two of them had fought about it!

She sighed as she remembered the first time they'd spoken. He'd phoned her from somewhere in South America after Janine had told him she was pregnant and planning to marry. He'd called Tom every name under the sun. Unable to fly home immediately as he was under contract to finish a mining job, he'd demanded that Mallory talk the couple out of getting married. She had refused.

He'd been furious. He'd phoned her several times over the next few days, but she'd remained firm. Tom wanted to marry Janine and as far as she was concerned, that was the end of it. Her brother had always had a good head on his shoulders and she had the utmost faith in both him *and* his good judgment of people.

She hadn't actually met Jordan Caine till the day of the wedding. She'd been dreading that first meeting, but to her surprise, his attitude had been nonconfrontational.

Only later had he revealed his true colours.

The reception had been held at a lakeside hotel outside Seattle, and after Tom and Janine had left for their honeymoon, Mallory had been feeling weepy. She'd stolen away from the party, and had walked down to the beach.

The evening was late but the summer air was still warm. She'd thought herself totally alone as she'd stood gazing out over the moon-lit waters—until she'd heard Jordan Caine's voice come harshly from behind her.

''I'll never forgive you.''

She'd turned, her heart thumping wildly against her ribs. He was standing a few feet away, his tux jacket shoved back by hands fisted on his hips as he glared at her.

She blinked away the tears that had been blurring her gaze, and tried to gather herself together. But before she could respond, he went on,

''Your brother should be locked up! My sister's only eighteen—for heaven's sake, she's just finished high school! He took advantage of her, got her pregnant, it's an absolute disgrace—''

"They're married now. Can't you just accept that?"

"She's just a baby herself! She could have had the child adopted—''

"Janine *desperately* wanted to keep her baby—''

"She's immature! She's hardly able to look after herself—''

"Tom will look after them both.'' Mallory kept her voice steady despite a spurt of anger. "You need have no worries about Janine…or the baby.''

"Dammit, you're every bit as stubborn and irresponsible as he is! If you'd backed me up, this wedding would never have taken place. My sister could have had the baby adopted and then gone on with her life—''

"She *is* getting on with her life. And it's going to be a good life. Tom starts work in Seashore when they come back from their honeymoon, and they've rented a lovely house there, for next to nothing. They were lucky, I admit. If it hadn't been available, they'd have had to settle for a basement suite…but still, they'd have been happy, because they're in love—''

A seagull suddenly swooped by the bedroom window, snapping Mallory back to the present.

She could hear footsteps in the room above. Was Jordan packing his things? Getting ready to leave? She hoped so. But she also prayed that before he left, he'd reassure her that he wasn't going to sell the house. At least, not yet.

He *must* see things differently, now that he knew the baby was Janine's. No way would he want to be responsible for throwing his own sister's child out on the street.

With her heart in her mouth, Mallory went out into the front hall and as she heard his steps approach the landing, she breathlessly waited for Matthew's uncle to come down.

CHAPTER THREE

JORDAN gestured curtly towards the sitting room as he reached the foot of the stairs. "We'll talk in there."

Bossy, bossy! "Let's go out to the backyard patio," Mallory said. "It's such a lovely day. My bedroom window's open, I'll be able to hear Matthew if he wakes up."

He shrugged. "Fine."

He followed her as she led the way along to the kitchen. When she opened the outside door, a startled robin flew off the redwood deck and in a flash of orange, disappeared around the side of the house.

Mallory crossed to the middle of the spacious deck, where a bench and chairs were arranged around a rectangular wooden table. Taking a seat, she watched as Jordan strode over to the edge of the deck and looked out over the lawn.

"It's a big garden." He jammed his hands into the pockets of his shorts. "Must take quite a bit of upkeep."

"But it's wonderful for children. A nice flat lawn—and lots of shrubs and nooks for playing hide-and-seek."

"Looks as if it was professionally landscaped, but I remember it as being neglected. Everything overgrown."

"It was, but Tom soon licked it into shape. Elsa gave him some tips but he had a green thumb and everything he touched seemed to flourish."

Jordan still had his back to her and at mention of Tom his spine stiffened and she sensed a wall of hostility rise between them. He'd had a very low opinion of Tom and he obviously didn't care to listen to her praise him.

Well, too bad. She wasn't about to gloss over her brother's talents and accomplishments just because Jordan Caine had been so blinkered he hadn't appreciated the man his sister had married.

His expression was shuttered when he finally walked back across the deck.

She'd expected him to sit across from her but instead he came around and leaned his backside against the table beside her, so close that if she'd wanted to, she could have stroked

GRACE GREEN 49

his left thigh. A powerful, tanned, and brawny thigh. If she'd wanted to. Which, she decided as she determinedly raised her gaze, she most definitely did not!

He folded his arms across his chest and looked down at her. "Right," he said, "let's discuss our options."

She refocused her thoughts and waited.

"The first," he went on, "would be to put the kid up for adoption—"

"No." She didn't raise her voice. She just said "No," very quietly, but in an icy tone that made it clear that this was not, nor ever would be, an option.

"Okay, no surprise there. Next option, you keep him. You'd have sole custody."

She grasped the arms of her chair. "Naturally," she said, "this would be the option I'd choose."

"The only snag being, from your point of view, that you wouldn't have this house."

She'd hoped that the second option would include his letting her rent the house. Her spirits sank as she realized it did not. "That's a limited option," she said. "If I didn't have the house, the best I could afford would be a dingy basement apartment—''

''The third option,'' he plowed on, ''would be for me to have custody. I'd keep the house, of course, and—''

''*You?*'' Stunned, she stared at him. ''But you don't even like babies. You admitted that this morning. You said you didn't like babies and you wanted nothing to do with—''

''I didn't know, at that time, that we were talking about *Janine's* baby.'' His gray eyes had a steely glint. ''We're talking family here, Mallory. Family, blood ties—''

''But you said just now that the first option would be to have him adopted—''

''I threw that in for good measure. Like you, it wasn't something I'd have considered.''

Frantically, she tried to keep her cool. ''You're not being consistent. You originally wanted *Janine* to have him adopted—in fact, you were hell-bent on it! Now you say that one option would be for you to keep him yourself—''

''Apples and oranges. Yes, I wanted Janine to have her baby adopted, but only because she was too young and immature to take on the

responsibility of a child—and because she had
her whole life ahead of her. This scenario is
totally different. For me, money's no problem—and," he added drily, "at the grand old
age of thirty-five, my life's half over."

"But—"

"This baby is my only connection to Janine.
I want to be part of his life, and I want him to
be a part of mine."

"But you spend most of your time abroad!"

"No problem. I'd hire a nanny to care for
him while I'm out of the country—"

"A *nanny?*" Mallory's outraged expression
told him exactly what she thought of *that* idea.
"You'd leave Matthew with a stranger? No
way! I'll fight you in court if—"

"The fourth option," he interjected
smoothly, "would be for the two of us to share
custody."

She gave a derisive—and most unladylike—
snort. "You're joking, of course!"

"Do I look as if I'm joking?"

He did not. His jaw was clamped, his lips
compressed, his gray eyes hard as cement.

"Us? Sharing custody?" She shook her
head. "Uh-uh. It would never work. We would
never get along—"

"Why not?"

"Your attitude, for one thing."

"What's wrong with my attitude?"

"You're arrogant and rude and controlling and—"

"You're stubborn and bloody-minded," he growled. "And far too romantic for your own damned good!"

"Romantic?" Where the heck had that come from!

"You're looking at this situation through rose-tinted glasses—it's as if you'd found a baby on your doorstep and you see the two of you living together and being happy ever after. The reality is, you can barely afford to keep him. The reality is a child is better off with two parents."

"The reality is that he'd be far better off with one than with two people who'd be sparring constantly the way you and I do! And besides, shared custody would be so unsettling for Matthew it would make his little head spin. He'd have to move back and forth between us, never knowing a real home."

"Of course he'd know a real home!" Jordan's voice was rough with impatience. "If we were to share custody, you'd stay on in this house.''

Totally taken aback, she stared at him. After several beats, she said, ''And you? Where would you fit in?''

''I'd continue with my work abroad but we'd share responsibility for the baby, make joint decisions regarding his welfare. And I'd visit when I could.''

She chewed her lip. ''You'd consider this your...home?''

''Uh-uh. Home is where I hang my hat.'' His grin was self-mocking. ''And I never wear a hat.''

Looking at him warily, Mallory said, ''You'd be happy to leave Matthew with me?''

''I don't recall using the word *happy*. Let's just say, you'd be right for the job. And he likes you.''

''But *you* don't.''

''It wouldn't be necessary for *me* to like you, Mallory. Or for you to like me.'' His gaze narrowed as he searched her face for an answer. ''You'd consider it? I myself see shared custody as the best option.''

"I'd prefer to have sole custody," she said stubbornly.

"Even without this house?"

"I could manage."

"As you yourself just said, if you didn't have this house, all you'd be able to afford would be some dingy basement apartment. But if you were determined to seek sole custody, we'd end up in court...and I'd win hands down."

"Oh, not necessarily," she shot back. "Just because you've got pots of money—"

"Pots of money can buy the best lawyers in the country. You wouldn't have a hope in hell of beating me." His smile was faintly malicious. "It's my turn, sweetheart. You won hands down when it came to the wedding; I'll beat you hands down when it comes to the baby. Seems only fair."

"You don't care about Matthew, do you! All you care about is winning!"

"But I think you'll agree with me, when you simmer down, that shared custody is the best option."

She drew in a very deep breath. "I agree," she said reluctantly, "that it's worth considering."

"Good. Because even though I know I'd win a custody battle, I'd prefer not to go that route. It wouldn't be in Matthew's best interests; he'd be better off with both of us looking after his welfare. Furthermore, as I said, he's used to you, and for his sake it would be better to hire you than hire a stranger to look after him."

"Hire me?" She gaped at him. "*Hire* me?"

"Weren't you paying attention? I said, you'd be right for the job, and 'job' is what I meant. You stay in the house, rent-free, and I pay you—well, whatever good nannies get paid." He pushed himself off the table and towered over her. "Take it or leave it, Mallory. That's the deal."

She sprang to her feet and glared up at him. "And what happens if you decide to get married? You'd have me out on the street in two seconds flat."

His grin was lazy. "Not a problem, sweetheart. I don't plan on marrying. Ever."

"That's what you say now. But how do I know that somewhere down the road you won't meet somebody, fall in love, and all of a sudden there's a new bride at Number Five

Seaside Lane. Somebody who loves children and doesn't want me around! No." She squared her shoulders rigidly. "I won't do it. I won't risk it."

"I'd be taking that chance too, Mallory. You don't have the resources at present to fight me in court...but what if you were to meet some millionaire and get married?"

"I have no plans," she said coldly, "to marry. Millionaire or no millionaire."

"That's what you say now." In a flat tone, he echoed her own words. "And I'm not prepared to risk it either."

As they stared at each other, Mallory felt a sinking sensation. "It seems," she said defeatedly, "that we've reached an impasse. I don't trust you, and you don't trust me."

"Then we'll just have to sign a contract. Make it legal. I don't marry; you don't marry."

"I don't think that would stand up in any court."

He sighed. "Probably not. Look." He rubbed the heel of one hand over his beard, making a rasping sound. "We can *make* this work. Trust me. I promise you, I'm not going to marry. I don't want a wife. I don't want to be tied down.''

''I'd like to believe you, but people change—''

''For God's sake, Mallory, what do I have to do to convince you?''

She drew in a deep breath. ''I don't know,'' she said. ''I don't know what you could do to convince me. But I could never agree to shared custody unless I have absolute faith that any agreement between us would be absolutely rock solid and permanent. I need that security. Because of Matthew. I love him too much to take any chances.''

Jordan walked away from her, back to the edge of the deck, and looked out over the garden again.

The robin had returned. It ran about the lawn, halting every few seconds to cock its head and look around with its sharp inquisitive eyes. Mallory watched it, her own gaze slightly blurred, her heart filled with despair. She and Jordan had, indeed, reached an impasse.

And she could see no way out.

She was standing there dismally, when she heard the phone ring inside.

She made her way to the kitchen and picked up the handset from the wall phone.

"Hello," she said. "Mallory Madison speaking."

"This is Celia, Ms. Madison, at Burton Barton Realty. May I speak to Mr. Caine?"

"Mr. Caine's outside. Could you hold on a minute, please, and—"

"I'm here."

Mallory turned and saw Jordan coming into the kitchen. She held out the phone. "It's Burton Barton Realty."

He nodded, and murmured "Thanks' as he took the phone. Then he said, "Jordan Caine here. Oh, hi, Celia…"

He listened for a few moments, before saying, "Two o'clock it is." Replacing the receiver, he announced, "Burton has a client coming to see the place at two."

Mallory leaned back against the countertop, glad of its support as her legs had become weak. "Word travels fast."

"It's a prime property, in a prime location."

"I guess."

"Celia suggested we take off when they're here. It's inhibiting for the client when the occupants are around."

"We'd better have a quick lunch, then, and once we're done, I'll feed Matthew."

Forcing herself to move, Mallory walked to the fridge. "It's not going to be anything very fancy. I brought enough food from Seattle for Matthew, but I haven't had time to do the rest of my grocery shopping—I'll go to the super-market when Burton and his client come. Elsa's left me some deli meat and buns, though. We can have ham sandwiches."

While they ate lunch, Mallory said—hardly daring to hope, "Have you given up your plan to fight me for Matthew?"

"What makes you think that?"

"You said that if you had custody of Matthew, you'd keep the house. And you also said that if we agreed to shared custody, you'd keep the house. Now since you've gone back to your original plan to sell, I have to deduce that you've counted both those options out. Does that mean you've given up your plan to fight me for him?"

"No," he said. "I intend to fight you for Matthew…"

Mallory had just taken a small bite of her sandwich; as he spoke she almost choked on it.

"...and I'll win. But I've had second thoughts about keeping the house. It'll be handier for me if Matthew's closer to an airport. That way, when I fly in from overseas, I won't have to waste time driving all the way to Seashore. I'll buy a condo in Seattle. Downtown."

"A *condo? Downtown?*" Mallory glowered at him. "Jordan Caine, you don't know the first thing about bringing up children! A little boy needs a backyard, a place to play safely outside—"

"The nanny can take him to a park." His tone was careless. "He'll survive. Other kids do."

Stomach churning, Mallory put down her sandwich and said scornfully, "You claim to have Matthew's interests at heart. I don't believe you. All you care about is getting back at me. You know how you'll hurt me if you take Matthew from me, and you'll take the greatest pleasure out of that. You really are contemptible!"

"Tut, Mallory, watch your blood pressure." His eyes had a taunting gleam as they fixed on her topknot. "Hair that colour..." He shook his head and looked as if he was trying to control laughter. "Quite a liability."

"Not such a liability as being born without a heart!" she snapped back. "And that's such a cliché," she added in a scathing tone, "about red hair—" But before she could go on, the front doorbell chimed.

Pushing back her chair, she rose abruptly to her feet and stalked from the kitchen. The man was unbearable. She was glad to escape his presence...and his juvenile humour!

When she opened the front door, she found Elsa standing on the stoop. Her neighbour's petite figure was neatly attired in a pink-and-white spotted dress. Her silver hair sparkled in the sunlight, and her eyes glowed with warmth.

"I've brought something for your dinner." She indicated the covered Pyrex bowl in her hands. "A chicken casserole. I saw the moving van and I knew you'd be busy, what with having company and unpacking all your boxes."

"Oh, thanks, Elsa. You're a godsend."

"How are things going?"

Mallory rolled her eyes. "Don't even ask!"

"That bad?"

"I was about to strangle him when you rang the bell!"

"I'll leave you to it, then."

"Come in and meet him—see for yourself how infuriating he is."

"I don't want to disturb—are you eating lunch?"

"No, we've finished."

"Then I'll come in, for just a minute." Elsa stepped inside. "Is Matthew having his nap?"

"He is," Mallory said. But as they passed the bedroom door, she heard a banging sound from inside. "He was!"

Chuckling, she and Elsa went into the bedroom and crossed to the crib. Matthew was lying on his back, hitting his fist against the bars.

The moment he saw them he beamed.

"Oh, look!" Elsa said with delight, "I think that first tooth has finally come through."

Mallory scooped him up and as she cradled him in her left arm, she checked his mouth. When she saw a sliver of white in his lower gum, she ran a fingertip lightly over it and felt the sharp edge.

"You're right, Elsa!" she exclaimed, and gave Matthew a hug. "Oh, what a clever boy you are! Now let's get you something to eat."

In the kitchen, they found Jordan slotting dishes into the dishwasher.

Keeping Matthew tucked against her shoulder so he couldn't see his uncle, Mallory said, "Elsa, I'd like you to meet Janine's brother, Jordan Caine. Jordan, this is Elsa Carradine."

Jordan straightened and stuck out his right hand. "Hi, Elsa. How are you?"

"Oh, I'm well, thanks. And you?"

"Couldn't be better," he said pleasantly.

Mallory ground her teeth. The man could be so darned plausible, with that open smile. But she knew him better...

"My condolences, Jordan, on losing your sister," Elsa said. "Janine was a very sweet girl. In the short time we knew her, everyone around here grew to love her."

"Thank you, Elsa. I appreciate hearing that."

"Matthew's so like her. Oftentimes a baby takes after both parents, but I see nothing of Tom in him."

Mallory felt a rush of panic. She had to cut Elsa off, before this dangerous line of conversation went any further.

"Elsa, would you pop the casserole in here and then I'll get Matthew's lunch ready?" She opened the fridge door as she spoke.

Elsa slid the dish into the fridge and then held out her arms for the baby. "Let me strap him into his chair."

"Thanks." She handed over the baby. "Just don't let him see Jordan. He's terrified of that beard." Weak with relief as she saw Elsa focus on Matthew, Mallory swept her suit jacket off the high chair where she'd draped it that morning, and turned the chair so it faced away from Jordan. "There, pop him in. I'm going to hang my jacket up."

As Mallory left the room, Jordan lounged against the counter and watched Elsa strap the baby into his high chair. Matthew obviously adored her. Though Jordan could see only the back of the baby's head, he could see the child's chubby little hands reach up, could hear him gurgle happily to her. And Elsa just as clearly adored Matthew. Her face was wreathed in smiles, her voice loving as she chatted to him.

'What a good boy,'' she said, ''to get your first tooth. And so clever, to get all that fussing over with before Auntie arrived, so you won't be keeping her up at night and she can have the nice rest she so richly deserves.''

Mallory came back into the kitchen and Jordan transferred his attention to her as she heated a small container of baby food in the microwave, and fastened a bib around the baby's neck, murmuring affectionately to the child while Elsa took a seat and watched dotingly.

Jordan hid a smug smile. He didn't like to think of himself as being manipulative, but he'd undoubtedly pressed one of Mallory's hot buttons when he'd oh-so-casually announced he intended to buy a condo in downtown Seattle.

He intended to do no such thing.

He had no intention of uprooting Matthew from his familiar surroundings and friends. He had no intention of hiring a stranger to look after the child. And he had no intention of selling the house. But her outraged response to his announcement had been exactly what he'd counted on.

By fair means or foul, by emotional black-mail if necessary, he'd persuade her to agree to shared custody. She didn't trust him, and he had no way of forcing her to. But if his ma-nipulations worked, she'd agree to his plan in the end, because she wanted what was best for Matthew.

As he himself did.

Janine's baby was his nephew and his re-sponsibility, and he was not a man who shirked responsibility. But Mallory was not only willing but desperate to take on that re-sponsibility too.

The baby was her Achilles' heel. And he felt no compunction about taking advantage of that vulnerability, because the end would justify the means. He needed someone reliable to look after Matthew while he was working abroad.

And Mallory Madison would make the per-fect nanny.

After Mallory had fed Matthew, Elsa said,
"Why don't I take him with me for a while? It'll give you a chance to unpack without him

getting into everything. All those boxes out in the front hall..."

"Thanks, Elsa," Mallory said tautly. "But I won't be unpacking. I discovered this morning that Number Five belongs to Jordan, and he has put it up for sale."

Elsa turned an astonished face to Jordan. "This is *your* house?"

He nodded.

"Did Janine and Tom know?"

"No," Mallory said. "He didn't want them to."

Elsa's eyes were thoughtful as she looked again at Jordan. "In my humble opinion, that was a very generous thing to do. Such good deeds are few and far between today. And the secret acts of kindness are the most worthy of all."

Mallory felt as if her staunchest ally had taken a step into the enemy's camp. But then Elsa went on, "Why are you selling now, though? What's Mallory going to do?"

"I appreciate your concern, Elsa," Jordan said casually. "But we'll work something out. Something that's in Matthew's best interests. In the meantime, I appreciate your offer to baby-sit. We need to clear the front hall before Burton Barton comes along at two with his client.''

''Someone's coming already?'' Elsa scooped the baby from the high chair. ''Well, in that case, I'll be pleased to take this little precious with me!'' She said her goodbyes to Jordan, and then walked with Mallory to the front hall.

As Mallory hauled Matthew's stroller from the closet, Elsa whispered, ''What on earth are you going to do now?''

''I don't know.'' Mallory strapped the baby into the stroller. ''He says he's going to fight me for custody…and win. And then he's going to buy a condo in downtown Seattle and hire a nanny to look after Matthew!''

''Oh, dear, how dreadful!''

''Dreadful doesn't even begin to describe it, Elsa. The man is despicable. He's not only despicable, he's—''

''He's what, sweetheart?''

Mallory spun around. Jordan was standing beside her pine armoire, his hands in his pockets, his eyes taunting. His cocksure attitude made her blood boil. And despite knowing that she'd do best not to antagonize him further, she threw caution to the winds and let her temper rip.

"You're despicable, Jordan Caine. Despicable and overbearing and heartless—"

She'd forgotten about Matthew. When she'd spun around so irately, she'd allowed the child a full view of his uncle. His uncle...and his uncle's black beard.

She'd no sooner hurled her insults at Jordan than Matthew spotted him. And without further ado, the baby opened his mouth wide and screamed blue murder.

Burton Barton arrived at two, just as Jordan was carrying the last box into the storage area next to the kitchen.

When the bell chimed, Mallory was in the sitting room. The last thing she wanted was for Jordan to sell the house, but though she'd have liked to thwart him, her conscience wouldn't let her. It was, after all, his house, and he had every right to sell it if he wanted. She cast a last quick glance around to make sure the room was tidy, and then with a heavy heart, she walked out to the front hall.

Jordan was on his way to the door. "I'll let them in," he said. "And then we'd better get out of here."

Mallory nodded and took off for her bedroom. Going into the ensuite bathroom, she patted a damp cloth over her face to cool her heated skin. She grimaced when she saw that her topknot was coming undone. After a brief hesitation, she decided it would be easier to let her hair down than fix it, so she unpinned the topknot, and ran her brush through the auburn curls till they crackled.

Then she moved back into the bedroom and crossed to the dresser by the door. As she retrieved her shoulder bag, she heard a strident female voice in the front hall.

"I'm very familiar with the property, Mr. Caine—I was a frequent visitor to the house when the Prentices owned it. As you say, both the house and location are ideally suited to running a B and B—except that there's not enough parking space in the drive so I'd have to pave over the backyard."

Mallory gasped in horror. Pave over that lovely garden? Unthinkable!

"And since it's already May," the woman went on haughtily, "immediate occupancy would be *essential*."

"No problem." Jordan's tonc was affable. "Now if you'll excuse me, I'll leave Burton to show you around."

Mallory swayed as panic threatened to overcome her. Things were moving too fast. Fragments of her earlier discussion with Jordan tumbled around in her mind, leaving her dazed as she struggled to sort out her options.

But what it boiled down to, really, was that if she wanted Matthew to live with her, she'd have to agree to shared custody. She couldn't afford to fight Jordan in court; and she couldn't *bear* to hand Matthew to a nanny—

Jordan appeared in her doorway. "Let's go."

She followed like a robot as he headed for the kitchen. He opened the back door and stood aside to let her go out.

Together they walked across the yard to the side gate. "It's a done deal," he said in a satisfied tone as he closed the gate behind them and emerged onto the drive. "Mrs. Trent said she'd had her eye on Number Five for years and was all set to present an offer for it last summer when I snatched it out from under her.'' He stopped at the Lexus. ''You said you were going to the supermarket. Where's your car?''

''In the garage. Wait!'' Mallory grabbed his arm as he took out his keys. ''I've thought things over,'' she said desperately. ''And I've changed my mind. I've decided to go along with your proposal that we share custody of the baby.''

CHAPTER FOUR

JORDAN barely managed to suppress an elated *YES!*

His strategy had worked. He had won.

"Despite the risks?" He quirked an eyebrow and regarded Mallory with a studied air of equanimity.

She dropped her hand. "I'll take that chance."

He had counted on it. "Okay. Let's take a walk along the beach and hammer out the details."

Grasping her arm, he didn't release it till after he'd propelled her across the wide street to the beach.

The ocean breeze was gusty and as they tromped over the salt grass and among the dunes, he noticed that it swept Mallory's hair back from her face in a tawny tumble.

Despite his aversion to redheads, he found himself intrigued by her vivid colouring.

It was amazing how everything toned in— the glossy auburn hair, the gracefully arched eyebrows, the chestnut brown eyelashes. In the bright sunlight, he noticed for the first time that tiny freckles adorned each high cheekbone— like finely ground nutmeg sprinkled on smooth fresh cream.

He noticed too that her face was strained, the pale skin tautly drawn.

The uncertainty over Matthew had taken its toll. But if her brother hadn't seduced Janine, the present situation wouldn't have existed. She'd obviously spoiled Tom rotten while she was bringing him up and if he then took what he wanted, willy-nilly, as an adult, she had only herself to blame for the problems he had left in his wake.

"You're happy with option four, then?" he asked.

"I don't recall using the word *happy!*" Her brown eyes had a sardonic gleam as she tossed his own earlier words back at him. "I still don't trust you, but I'm willing to accept your plan for shared custody. Except..."

He stopped walking, and frowned down at her. "Except what? Look, if you're going to start quibbling—"

"I won't take your money." She rubbed her palms down the side of her shorts as if they'd become clammy. "You won't *hire* me. He's Janine's baby but I love him as if he were my own. I won't be his nanny. I'll be his mother."

"You'll accept a paycheque or we don't have a deal." His tone was hard: *Take it or leave it.*

"Then I'll put it in a trust fund for Matthew!"

"You can toss it into the bloody ocean, for all I care." He shifted his feet impatiently. "That's it, then?"

"One other thing. I won't be a kept woman. It's your house, but I'll continue to pay the contracted rent."

He opened his mouth to nix her suggestion but then thought better of it. Her shoulders were rigidly set, her hands twisted together. She was like a spring too-tightly wound, he reflected. Any more stress and she'd break.

He didn't want a nanny on Prozac.

"Fine, pay the rent." It was a piddling amount anyway. "If it's necessary for your feeling of independence."

"It is."

"Then I'll concede that point. Okay, Mallory Madison." He offered his right hand. "You've got yourself a deal."

After a brief hesitation, she held out her hand. As he clasped it, he found the slender fingers surprisingly strong. Strong, yet fine-boned and feminine. He was struck by a sudden urge to pull her close and plant a kiss on that pouty mouth. Which would, he knew, be one huge mistake…

As she withdrew her hand and raised it to thrust back a clump of bouncy curls that the breeze had lolloped forward, he fought another temptation, this time to thread his own fingers through that gloriously sexy tawny mane.

Clearing his throat, he switched his focus to more practical matters. "This job you gave up in Seattle—what was it?"

"I worked at the Patterson Smythe Accounting firm."

"So you plan to set up your own accounting business?"

"If you'd forced me out of the house, yes, that's what I would have done. But it wouldn't have been my choice. I never did want to be an accountant," she confessed, "but math al-

ways came easily to me so when a career coun-
sellor from Patterson Smythe came to our high
school in my final year and offered me a job
after graduation—with on-the-job training—I
took it because I had...I had obligations.''

''You had Tom.'' Even saying the name ir-
ritated Jordan. ''Since your father couldn't
keep a job for two days on end, it was left to
you to keep the family together.''

''You make it sound as if caring for Tom
was a hardship,'' Mallory said stiffly. ''It
wasn't. I was twelve when our mother died,
but he was only five. He was lost and heart-
broken. I tried to make up for it—''

''And spoiled him rotten in the process.''

''I did *not* spoil him! He was a nice kid and
a responsible kid—oh, there's no point in discussing this with you. Where Tom's concerned, your mind is closed.''

Damned right it was. But as she said, there
was no point in discussing it. He moved on.
''What's this new career you've planned out
for yourself?''

''I'm going to run a family day care centre.
The house and garden are ideal for it, and I've

applied for all the necessary permits. So far everything looks fine.''

The woman was organized, he had to give her that.

''But first,'' she went on, ''I want to spend a month or two with Matthew and get him settled into a regular routine, so he'll feel secure with me before I bring other children into our lives.''

A household of screaming kids. Jordan shuddered. If he'd needed a reason to make his future visits to Seashore few and far between, this was it.

''I'd have thought,'' he said dryly, ''given that you had to spend your teen years—and beyond—looking after your brother, that you'd have soured yourself on kids forever!''

''On the contrary,'' she retorted, ''caring for Tom made me realize what a fulfilling job child-minding is. Besides, I enjoy having people around, especially children. They keep one young.''

''Personally,'' he rejoined, ''I can't think of anything that would age a person more rapidly!''

"You must spend some time with Matthew before you leave. That will surely change your mind."

"I think not." Who could enjoy spending time with a baby? Babies couldn't talk and as far as he was concerned, one-sided conversations were for dentists and drunks.

"When *are* you planning to leave?"

"On Monday, after I've talked with a lawyer and had him write a contract laying out what we've just agreed on."

Mallory looked at her watch. "I should get along to the supermarket now, and then pick Matthew up. I don't want to tire Elsa. Her son and daughter-in-law are arriving tomorrow for a visit. She's going to be busy."

As they started up the beach, Jordan said, "Do you have a bank account here?"

"Not yet."

"While you're in town, open one up so I can deposit your checks on a monthly basis."

"Are you going back now to tell Burton the property's no longer for sale?"

"No, I'll go along to his office later."

"And in the meantime," Mallory asked anxiously, "what if that woman tenders an offer you can't refuse?"

"There's no amount she could possibly offer," Jordan returned grimly, "that would persuade me to sell to a person who planned to turn that garden into a damned parking lot!"

Mallory walked along the aisle at the SureBuy supermarket, her mind elsewhere as she added items to her grocery basket.

She'd been right about Jordan Caine. He had no real interest in Matthew. Oh, he was determined to be in control of the situation, but his declaration that he wanted to be part of the child's life was an empty one. It was clear that he couldn't wait to get out of Seashore.

And just as well. She'd spoken the truth when she'd told him that working with him would be difficult. Their values were different; their approaches were different. When she saw someone in need, she gave from the heart. When Jordan Caine saw someone in need, he gave from the wallet.

It was the depth of that wallet which troubled her now as she mulled over their deal. It seemed solid enough yet it had left her with a vague sense that she'd been duped—that Jordan had somehow put one over on her. She couldn't pin it down. All she knew was, she didn't trust him.

How could she be *sure* that one day he wouldn't marry and try to take Matthew from her?

She sighed. What was the point in worrying about something that might never happen? She banished all her negative thoughts and concentrated on her shopping.

The store wasn't busy and within minutes she was out in the parking lot again, headed for her Honda. After packing away her groceries, she walked to the street, and was halfway to the bank when she heard someone call her name.

Turning, she saw Tyler Scott striding towards her along the sidewalk. Tyler was the youngest doctor at the town's new medical clinic—and a snazzy dresser who was looking particularly elegant today in an exquisitely-cut linen suit.

He greeted her with a delighted smile. "Mallory, wonderful to see you!"

"Hi, Tyler." Mallory squinted against the sun as she looked up at him. "I'm surprised you're not out sailing on such a glorious day!"

"I wish!" he said. "But I'm on call this weekend. So, you've finally made the break. How's it going?"

She could have told him of all the complications that had arisen, but decided not to detail her personal problems. Tyler had made it clear, on the occasions when she'd taken Matthew to the clinic for his needles, that he'd like to get to know her better. She wasn't interested. She didn't want to offend him, though; it would be awkward, since he was Matthew's doctor.

"Everything's going well," she said lightly. "The movers arrived this morning and I'm going to start unpacking when I get back. Elsa's looking after Matthew—which reminds me, I'd better get going!" She made to move on, but he touched her arm to detain her.

"Would you like to sail some afternoon?"

"Thanks, but I'm going to be busy for the next while, getting the house ready for my day care. And looking after Matthew. And the garden, of course, is going to require—"

"Enough already!" He laughed. "Okay, you can't blame a guy for trying." Something of her embarrassment must have shown in her face because he added, "Don't look so *worried,* Mallory! It's not the first time I've been brushed off and it won't be the last. We can still be friends."

She looked at him doubtfully.

"I promise!" He gazed at her solemnly but his eyes twinkled as he pressed his manicured hand to his heart.

She smiled. "All right. Friends."

"And you'll come sailing with me sometime, now that we've sorted that out? You can bring Matthew along."

"That would be fun," she said. And she knew it would.

As she hurried away, a flash of colour caught her eye. Turning her head, she saw Jordan's scarlet Lexus drive past.

He didn't see her.

Or, if he did, he made a good job of pretending not to!

Jordan was gone for a couple of hours, and when he returned to Number Five, he found the house quiet.

Wandering through to the kitchen, he saw Mallory out on the deck, in her shorts and

T-shirt, her feet bare. She was pinning tiny shirts and diapers onto a pulley clothesline.

On the lawn, in the shade of an apple tree, was a playpen. In it Matthew lay on his back, waving a rattle.

Jordan focused his attention on Mallory as she leaned over to catch up the last diaper from the laundry basket.

She did have *great* legs, he mused. And a sexy rear end. She also had a tiny waist, slender hips...and as she reached up to hang the diaper on the line, he noted that though her breasts were small enough that he could have cupped them easily in his palms, they were round and resilient—and the upthrusting movement outlined taut peaks that pressed against the thin fabric of her T-shirt.

He felt a tug of desire.

Dammit. He scowled bad-temperedly. That was the last thing he needed, to lust after this woman...

Heck, he didn't even like redheads!

But his aversion to them was obviously not shared by that blond lady-killer she'd been cosying up to on the sidewalk. He'd looked as if he wanted to eat her...and she'd looked as if she'd have been more than happy to be on his plate.

The guy had also looked as if he had money. The suit he'd been sporting—an Armani?— must have cost big bucks...

But how *much* money did he have?

Enough to subsidize Mallory in a child custody case?

Jordan scraped a hand over his beard as he mulled the matter over. Mallory had insisted he could trust her. But could he?

Suspicion gnawed at him as she came inside.

"Oh, hi," she said pleasantly. "You're back. How did it go? Did you get everything sorted out with Burton?"

"Yeah. Mrs. Trent hadn't put in her offer yet, so that simplified things." He poured cold water into a glass. "How about you? Did you get to the bank?"

"Yes. I've written down the branch name and address and my account number and put a copy upstairs in your room."

"Good." He swallowed a mouthful of water and then said, in a deliberately vague tone, "I thought I saw you talking to some guy over by the supermarket...?''

''Dr. Scott. He's Matthew's doctor.''

Aha! A doctor: a high earner. ''You know him well?''

''Oh, sure, I've always taken the baby to Tyler for his shots and checkups.''

So Mallory and the good doctor were on a first-name basis.

''I'd never looked after a baby before,'' she added, ''and I didn't have much confidence at first. I asked Tyler a lot of questions. He was very understanding.''

''So how's your confidence level now?''

''Much better.'' She opened the fridge door and took out Elsa's chicken casserole. ''But I'm lucky Tyler's so helpful.''

''He looks young.''

''He's a couple of years older than I am.''

''He looks...prosperous.''

Switching on the oven, she took potatoes and carrots from a cupboard, and a peeler from the cutlery drawer. ''Excuse me,'' she said. ''I need to use the sink.''

He moved aside. ''Why did the doc choose to work in Seashore?'' He tried to sound as if he were just making idle conversation. "It's such a backwater."

"He inherited a yacht from his godfather a few years ago—The Silver Lining—which was docked here at our local marina. Tyler made a flying trip from Chicago, intending to check the vessel out and sell it, but he fell in love with both the yacht and the area. After that, he vacationed here every chance he could. When a position opened up at the new medical clinic, he was in there like Flynn. He works hard but he plays hard too. Sailing's his passion."

"An expensive passion."

Mallory rinsed the peeled potatoes and started on the carrots. "Fortunately for Tyler, he not only inherited the yacht, he also inherited his godfather's fortune."

A fortune, no less! "So," he said, "have you been out on the boat?"

"I'm going to have my first sail soon." She finished scraping the carrots and after running them under the tap, she made for the door. "I'm going to bring Matthew in for dinner. Could you make yourself scarce? Your beard…"

Jordan put his glass in the dishwasher and then glanced out the window, in time to see Mallory sweep the kid up from the playpen. The child tried to catch hold of her hair while she drew her head back and laughed.

They made an attractive picture.

Feeling oddly reluctant to move, he watched as they approached the house. And he remained there, at the window, till Mallory stepped up onto the deck.

Then he jerked to life. Wheeling around he strode out of the kitchen. He had no interest in seeing the kid—nor had he any interest in instigating another screaming fit!

''He's gone, sweetheart.'' Mallory tucked Matthew into his high chair. ''And thank goodness. You don't want to see that bristly black beard again, *do* you!''

She fed the child and then took him to his room for a nap. When she returned to the kitchen to get dinner organized, she found Jordan there, opening a bottle of white wine. On the island sat two of the crystal wineglasses someone had given Tom and Janine as a wedding present.

"What's the occasion?" she asked.

"No occasion." He poured the wine. "My contribution towards dinner. I picked it up when I was in town."

Mallory reached for an oven mitt. "It'll go nicely with the chicken." She opened the oven door and withdrew the vegetables and Elsa's casserole. "It's hot in here—would you like to eat outside, on the patio?"

"I've already set the picnic table."

She raised her eyebrows. "You're surprisingly domesticated."

"Heaven forfend!" he said in mock horror. "What I am is self-sufficient."

She dished out their meal and carried the plates outside, while Jordan followed with their wine.

"Did you start your unpacking?" he asked as they took their seats across from each other at the table.

"I meant to, but I got so caught up with playing with Matthew I didn't get around to it." She took a sip of her wine. "Mmm, this goes down smoothly! Anyway, I'll unpack a box or two after dinner, and leave the rest till tomorrow. Where did you get to, after you picked up the wine?''

He toyed with his dinner roll. "I took a drive to the cemetery.''

Mallory put down her glass. She felt as if a shadow had fallen over her heart. "I'm sorry. I should have offered to take you there earlier—''

"I preferred to go alone." He was silent again for a while. When he did speak, his voice had a husky quality. "It's a pretty spot. Peaceful.''

It was indeed. Occupying a gentle grassy slope on the outskirts of town, the graveyard overlooked the ocean and was situated away from the noise and bustle of the highway.

"I walk there with Matthew." She felt her eyes smart as she spoke. "And I talk to him…about Tom and Janine.''

"You had a lot to cope with, on your own. I should have been there. For support.''

Mallory took in a deep breath. She had been angry about this, and for so long. He had given her an opening to confront him about it; she wasn't about to let it slide.

"So," she challenged, "why weren't you?''

Tension snapped into place between them, splintering the moment of rapport. "It wasn't possible."

"Because you were with some woman." Mallory didn't try to hide her resentment.

A nerve twitched under his right eye. "How did you know about that?" he demanded roughly.

"When I phoned the camp the second time, I was told you'd been seen taking off with some woman. Couldn't she have waited? Was she so important to you that you had to miss your own sister's *funeral?*"

"Yes." He picked up his glass and downed his wine in one long swallow. Then rubbing the back of his hand across his mouth, he put down the glass. "Just take my word for it." His tone was harsh. "End of story."

She opened her mouth to persist but the expression on his face chilled her. Stopped her. She felt a strange prickling at her nape. A warning prickle. It told her that nothing good would come from pursuing the subject.

She was reminded of his startling overreaction to the sharp *Ping!* of the toaster. His glittering stare on that occasion had made her feel exactly the way she felt now: that to press him for answers could actually be dangerous.

Suppressing a shiver, she lifted her fork and knife and focused her attention on her meal, eating every scrap although her appetite had fled. When her plate was empty, she polished off her wine. When she finally looked at Jordan again, she saw that his plate was empty and he was sitting back in his chair, his gaze fixed on her steadily.

"I've been thinking," he said.

His tone was mild. Taken aback by the sudden change in his attitude, she asked warily, "About what?"

"About us."

"Us?" The wine had gone to her head. She felt dizzy.

"Us...and Matthew."

"I thought we had all that settled?" She set her elbows on the table. "We're going to share custody. We're going to see a lawyer on Monday and sign a contract—"

"It's not enough."

She put her fingertips to her temples which had started to throb. "Not enough? But you said—"

"I've come up with another plan." His tone was as smooth as his wine. "A better plan."

Mallory felt a rush of panic. What was he trying to pull? Any change in plan—any change *he* came up with—would surely be to his advantage, not hers. "Go on."

"This new contract would be much more binding. And it will put all your doubts to rest, because if I were ever to break it, that would give you the upper hand in any subsequent custody case."

Mallory stiffened. This had to be a trick. "I can't think what you could possibly have come up with that would make me feel totally secure."

He got to his feet and rounded the table. He stood looking down at her, with his back to the low evening sun. The golden rays backlit him and gave him a halo—an angelic halo that was in stark contrast to his dark-bearded visage.

"What I propose," he said, "is a contract with no way out. No way out but…divorce." His eyes narrowed to silver slits as she uttered a little gasp. "What I'm proposing is that we get married."

Married? The shock of his proposal set her already dizzy mind spinning out of control.

"Uh-uh." She slumped back in her seat. "I've already told you. Marriage is not on my agenda."

"Nor was it on mine," he said with an impatient shake of his head. "But this marriage would be in name only. A contract. That's all. On paper. But the beauty of the arrangement would be this: it would lock us both in so neither of us would be free to marry anyone else."

She stared at him, trying to gather her thoughts as she let the full implication of his proposal sink in.

"Come on!" He rat-tatted his fingers against his thighs. "What do you think?"

Swallowing the lump in her throat, she rose to her feet and turning away from him, walked down to the bottom of the garden. How ironic it was that he had come up with the one scenario that would have given her peace of mind. But to become his wife? No way could she accept his proposal. It would be grossly unfair to him. It was one thing to act as a mother to Janine's baby; it was quite another thing—in view of the crucial information she was keeping from him!—to enter into a marriage founded on deception and lies.

It would be unforgivable.

She braced herself as he came up behind her.

"Look," he said, "I admit I had no time for Tom, but after all, he *was* the baby's father. Family, Mallory. Blood ties. We have an equal claim on the kid. Fifty-fifty. So…what do you say?"

Forcing all emotion from her expression, she turned to face him. "I say no."

"But marriage to me would safeguard your position—"

"I *can't* marry you."

His eyes became hard. Suspicious. Angry. "Why not? Do you have someone else in mind?"

"Of course not!"

"Then why won't you—"

"You'll just have to take my word for it," she said resolutely. "I *can't*. And I'm not about to tell you why."

She felt as if her conscience was being torn in two. She *should* tell him why, even though knowing the truth would give him the power to take Matthew from her...and that would break her heart. But she *couldn't* tell him why, because if she did, she'd be breaking the promise she'd made to Janine. The promise that had now come back to haunt her. The promise to keep the couple's shattering secret forever:

Tom was not the father of Janine's baby.

CHAPTER FIVE

JORDAN glowered at her. "Then we go back to the original plan and sign the shared custody contract on Monday?"

She nodded…and clumsily brushed a hand over her eyes. But not before he had seen the shine of tears.

Dammit, he hated to see a woman cry. Hated it because he hadn't a clue how to deal with it. He cleared his throat, and looked away.

Over the fence, he could see the ocean. The horizon was a hazy blue, violently streaked with crimson. He stared, entranced by the sheer beauty of it. No wonder Dr. Tyler Scott had fallen in love with this area—

"Excuse me," Mallory said in a tight voice as she sidestepped him. "I'm going inside to get our dessert."

He followed her slowly and found his gaze drawn to her hair as the sun's rays turned the rippling cascade to flame. Boy, that was something! He didn't like redheads but…

He couldn't seem to drag his eyes from this one. Couldn't keep them from her hair, her hips—and her long bare legs as they swung her gracefully into the house.

Drifting from a nearby garden came the lazy strum of a guitar, and a voice singing sadly of love and broken dreams.

The music touched something deep inside him and he felt his heart ache.

Just as his body ached.

How long was it since he'd had a woman?

Too damned long!

With a sudden and intense feeling of frustration, he stepped up onto the deck and found himself pacing back and forth on it, restlessly, until Mallory came outside again.

She set a tray on the table, bearing two mugs of coffee and their dessert.

"Chocolate marble cheesecake." With a casual smile, she pushed his plate across the table. "Enjoy."

She'd not only recovered her composure, she was offering an olive branch. He admired her for that; and he was more than ready to put an end to the hostilities.

"That's a helluva helping!" he growled, eyeing the calorie-laden dessert with misgivings as he took his seat. "What are you trying to do? Give me a heart attack?"

"Trying to put a bit of weight on you," she retorted. "You look as if you haven't had a decent meal in months."

She was right about that—not that he was about to tell her so. "It's the heat," he said vaguely. "It makes you lose your appetite..."

"Maybe I should try it sometime." Her tone was wry. "Just to get rid of those ever-elusive ten pounds..."

His attention was on the cheesecake, with its chocolate swirls. "If you have any extra pounds," he said, "don't worry about them. From what I've seen, they're in all the right places..." He threw her a casual glance and was surprised to see her cheeks had turned pink.

"No need to blush," he said as he picked up his spoon. "I'm not coming on to you. I'm just stating a fact. You have a fantastic figure." He waved the spoon at her. "This is where you're supposed to say 'Thank you'!"

He thought he saw a flicker of a smile. "Thank you."

"You're welcome." But his attention was once more on the cheesecake. He took a spoonful and closed his eyes as the confection melted in his mouth. "Oh this," he said, "is *wicked.*" He looked across at her again. "You made it?"

She nodded.

"Then you should be ashamed of yourself, creating such a temptation. A man might sell his soul for less."

"Not much of a soul if it could be had for a slice of cheesecake!"

He laughed. "You're right. But...maybe his heart. Don't they say that the way to a man's heart is—"

"I'm not interested," she said, "in finding the way to any man's heart. And as far as you're concerned, it's open to debate whether you even have one!"

"I'll let that slide," he said, with a sly smile. "I'm much more interested in knowing why you're a man-hater."

"I'm not a man-hater."

"Then why are you so against marriage?"

"Why are *you?*"

"Uh-uh, I asked first. Have you ever been in a serious relationship with a man?"

She stiffened. "That's none of your business."

He dropped his teasing attitude. "Mallory, what I know about you could be written on the back of a postage stamp. You're going to be bringing up my nephew so I think I should know something about your background—"

"Are you *interviewing* me?"

"I want to get a sense of who you are."

She toyed with her dessert for a moment, and then said, reluctantly, "I've had a couple of serious relationships."

"Long-term?"

"Yes."

"How about the more recent one?"

"We were together for four years."

"When did you split up?"

She slipped a spoonful of dessert into her mouth, and didn't answer till she'd eaten it. "Not too long ago."

"Want to tell me why?"

"We...had a major disagreement about something." She looked down at her plate. "I wouldn't give in.'' When she looked up again, her cheeks had become pale.

''Was the disagreement about Matthew?''

Surprise flickered in her eyes. ''Yes.''

''He didn't want the kid so he dumped you. What a b—''

''It wasn't like that—''

''Then tell me what it *was* like!''

''He—Nick Sullivan—has nothing against babies…it's just that he can't have them around. He's a writer. He needs absolute quiet or else he can't concentrate—''

''So he gave you an ultimatum.''

''And I gave him back his ring.'' She raised her coffee mug and he saw that her knuckles were white. ''The men in my life—starting with my father—always let me down in some way. After Nick…well, that's when I finally decided to go it on my own.''

''Are you still in love with him?''

''That *really* is none of your business!''

He held his palms up defensively. ''Sorry.''

She looked at him for a long moment, her lips thinned, and then she nodded. ''So…why have *you* never married?''

He pulled back his mouth in a grimace. "You're not going to like the answer to that question."

"Try me."

He shrugged. "I've always been able to get what I want without having to tie any knots."

"What you want, meaning…sex?"

"Yeah."

"If that's all you want from a woman, that's your choice. And it's none of *my* business!" She pushed aside her empty plate. "But what about love, companionship, commitment?"

"You think these things come automatically with marriage?" His laugh was cynical. "Honey, my parents' marriage was a battlefield—"

"Yes, I know. Janine told me they'd divorced when she was a baby and you were seventeen. But she also told me that your father remarried and his second marriage was a success. Didn't your stepmother welcome you both into their home?"

Oh, the seductive Arlene had welcomed him all right…but in ways that had left him with an intense aversion to redheads. His skin crawled as he recalled the repugnant advances his titian-haired stepmother had routinely made when his father wasn't around.

"Oh, the marriage was a great success." He kept his tone cool. "If you ignored the fact that Arlene cheated on my father every chance she got."

"Janine didn't mention that!"

"She didn't know."

A wind had arisen, and it gusted up over the lawn. The sun had gone down; the evening was cooling off. He saw Mallory shiver as she drank the last of her coffee.

He got to his feet. "Ready to go in?"

"Yes." She gathered up her dishes. "I'd like to start unpacking, but before I do, could you help move my furniture out of the storeroom? Some of it has to go upstairs and I won't be able to manage it on my own."

"Sure. Just tell me where you want it to go."

Mallory stood back and looked at the gold-framed oil painting Jordan had just hung above the sitting room mantelpiece. "A fraction more to the left," she said, then added quickly, "Stop, that's perfect!"

Jordan stepped off the raised hearth and moved back to join her. He idly swung the hammer in his hand as he glanced at the painting. "Looks good there."

"Just one thing left," she said. "My pine armoire."

"Where do you want it?"

"Upstairs, in the baby's bedroom."

"I thought the baby shared your room?"

"Oh, that was just a temporary arrangement—it was easier for me, when I was here only at the weekends, to close off the upstairs. Now that I'm here permanently, I'll move my things up to the master bedroom. I'll help you with the armoire. It's not too heavy, just awkward."

Awkward it was, but finally they managed to wrestle it upstairs and into the baby's room. It wasn't until after they'd set the armoire against the wall, that Jordan looked around the room. Mallory saw him raise his eyebrows.

"What a transformation! This was pretty drab last time I saw it. Bare walls, plank floor, no curtains…"

"It's lovely now, isn't it!" Mallory's eyes ran appreciatively over the azure carpet, the blue-and-white wallpaper, the white miniblinds in the bay window. "Janine had a flair for decorating and she chose the colours—Tom laid the carpet and did the painting and wallpapering."

She sat down on the cushioned window seat and smoothed her hands over the striped fabric. "Janine sewed these covers. She was a born homemaker." Her eyes misted at the memory. "You would have been proud of her, Jordan. She was so happy, getting everything ready for the baby."

"I *was* proud of her." Jordan's dark frown made him look ferocious. "She was a good kid."

"You meant everything to her. I know you didn't want her to get married, but despite that, you did attend her wedding and you really made her day—"

"Do you think I would have done anything to hurt her? She was the only person in the world that I cared about!"

Mallory heard anger in his voice, but behind the anger she heard pain.

"Jordan, I—"

''Excuse me,'' he said abruptly, ''I'm going out for a while.'' And turning on his heel, he strode from the room.

She heard him go down the stairs, heard him go out the front door. And a moment later she heard the roar of a car engine, and knew he'd taken off somewhere in his Lexus.

Her heart went out to him. She could well imagine how he was feeling. He'd loved Janine and seeing this room, which she'd prepared for Matthew, must be ripping him apart.

She wished there was something she could do to help him through this difficult time, but she knew there was not. He would have to muddle through it on his own.

Just as she was doing herself!

With a sigh, she went downstairs and along to the storeroom. After standing for a moment looking at the big cardboard boxes, she chose the one marked Dishes and hauled it into the kitchen.

She unpacked three boxes in all, and by the time she'd finished, it was after midnight, so she changed Matthew's diaper and then went to bed.

She lay awake, thinking about Jordan. Worrying about him. And she didn't manage to fall asleep until after she'd heard him coming in.

When Jordan woke up the next day, he found it was almost noon. He also found that Mallory had slipped a note under his door: Gone to Church.

Good. The house was empty.

After a quick shower, he dragged on a white T-shirt and a pair of black jeans and headed out of the bedroom.

He was halfway down the stairs, running his fingers through his damp hair, when the front door opened.

Mallory appeared…and the sight of her stopped him in his tracks.

She looked drop-dead gorgeous in a slip of a dress in some silky mocha fabric. Her hair was tied loosely back, and as she looked up at him, the russet curls glowed in the sunlight streaming down through the skylight. He felt as if he were hyperventilating…

"Ah," she said, "there you are!"

He gulped some air into his lungs even as he asked himself what the hell was happening to him. He'd never before had such a reaction to a woman...and especially to a woman who wasn't even his type.

Forcing his legs to move, he walked down the remaining steps. "Where's the kid?" he asked.

"He's out front, in his stroller." Her eyes flicked to his damp hair. "Did you just get up?"

"Guilty—but I guess I can put it down to jet lag. I'm on my way to have my break-fast—"

"Then I've caught you in time."

"For what?"

"Sam and Meg Grainger—the owners of the Seashore Inn—have invited us over there for brunch."

"Thanks," he said. "But I'll take a rain check. I'm not in the mood for company."

"Are you sure? Meg was awfully good to Janine—I thought you might like to meet her...and her husband—"

What kind of perfume was this woman wearing? Amber and Oriental. Sexy but in the most subtle of ways. Like a kiss in the dark. Disturbing. Distracting. Damned distracting.

Just as she herself was distracting. He wished she wouldn't look up at him like that, her brown eyes anxious, her lips pouty, her slim fingers pressed together under her chin as if in prayer.

He scowled. ''Look, I don't want to sound like Greta Garbo, but—''

''You vant to be alone!'' Her rueful smile brought a dimple to her right cheek—a dimple he found just as distracting as her perfume. Even as he stared at it, it winked out, and he was struck by a sudden urge to make her smile again, to bring the dimple back...

''I do understand,'' she was saying. ''I feel like that too, sometimes. Okay, then, I'll give your apologies—''

A brisk tap-tap at the open door interrupted her and Jordan saw a young woman hovering in the doorway. Tall and stylish, the stranger had close-cropped blond hair and an air of confidence. She was wearing a crisp cotton maternity dress the exact sky-blue of her eyes...

And those strikingly blue eyes were fixed on him with frank curiosity.

"Meg." Mallory made an inviting gesture. "Come in, meet Jordan."

Smiling, the blonde walked into the hall. "I just wanted to tell you to bring your swimsuits. We'll go down to the beach after brunch."

As Mallory made the introductions, Meg thrust out her hand. "Hi, Jordan. Pleased to meet you."

Jordan took her hand and was given a brief no-nonsense handshake. "Hi," he said, and finding himself subjected to her close appraisal, he grinned. "So," he drawled, "what's the verdict?"

The sky-blue eyes widened, and then he saw the cherry-pink lips quirk at the corners.

She slid her hands into the deep pockets of her dress and said, in an amused tone, "Mallory was wrong about you, Jordan Caine."

He raised his eyebrows.

"She said you were ferocious." The blonde chuckled and turned to her friend. "He's not *ferocious,* Mallory. The man's a pussycat!"

"Meg!" Mallory's tone was protesting, her cheeks flushed. She avoided looking at him.

"Sorry." Laughing, Meg gave Mallory a quick hug. "But you know me—always say what I think, no matter what. Well, I'd better take off before I get more deeply into hot water. And speaking of hot water," she added over her shoulder as she strode across the hall and out the door, "don't forget those swimsuits."

"Meg," Mallory called after her, "I'll be coming on my own…"

Too late. Meg had already gone.

"Ferocious, huh?"

At sound of Jordan's mocking words, Mallory stifled a frustrated mutter. Well aware of Meg's propensity for blunt speaking, she should've kept her opinion of him to herself. All she could do now was try to retrieve the situation.

She tossed back her hair and gave him her most supercilious look. *"Pussycat?"* she said in a tone of disbelief. "I don't *think* so!"

He laughed. The first genuine laugh he'd directed at her. And as the sound rang in her ears, her heart gave a startled lurch. In that moment, she'd caught a glimpse of a man she'd never seen before. A charming man. A man who could indeed, when it suited him, be a pussycat. His dark-lashed gray eyes glowed with an appreciative warmth that reached out and enfolded her. To her dismay, she realized how easy it would be to fall in love with Jordan Caine...

It was the last thing in the world that she wanted.

"Excuse me." Fighting a surge of panic, she bypassed him and made for the storeroom. "I have to get my bikini."

Once in the privacy of the storeroom, she took a deep breath and leaned, trembling, against the wall. She must not even let herself *think* that thought again! Falling in love with Jordan Caine could only lead to heartbreak. He was a "here today, gone tomorrow" kind of guy. He was a "take what I need, to hell with commitment" kind of guy. Exactly the kind of man she did *not* need in her life.

And she would do well to remember it. If she was looking for a husband, which she most definitely was not, Matthew's uncle wouldn't even make the short list. He could charm every bird out of every tree in the world, but no way was she going to let him charm her.

And with that decision firmly in her mind, she concentrated on rummaging through the cardboard box marked Summer, till she found her black bikini and her beach towel.

When she went out to the hall again, Jordan was still there.

"Find it?" he asked.

Ignoring the lilt of her pulse, she nodded.

He walked her out to the stoop and she saw that Meg and Sam had wandered away along the sidewalk, with Meg pushing Matthew in the stroller. The couple's son Andy was a few yards ahead of them, twisting and turning on his skateboard.

"That's Meg's husband?" Jordan asked.

"Sam. And their son Andy. He's fourteen."

The sun was high in the sky; the air warm and still. From the beach came the steady surging of the waves, the occasional cry of a wheeling gull.

Mallory dug into her bag for her sunglasses. "I should be back by five. How will you spend the afternoon?"

"I noticed the backyard fence has a couple of missing slats, and the attic window's broken. I'm going to check the rest of the place out," he said, "to see if anything else needs fixing. Then tomorrow, before I leave town, I'll get in touch with a contractor.''

''I'll see you around five, then.''

As Mallory walked away, Jordan's words echoed in her head: *before I leave town.*

For the past several months, she'd been looking forward to starting her new life here with Matthew. Jordan's unexpected arrival had turned her plans upside-down. But only temporarily. Tomorrow, thank goodness, he'd be gone.

''Did Caine tell you why he didn't come home for the funeral?''

''No, Sam.'' Mallory flicked beach sand from the skirt of her dress as she looked up at Meg's husband. ''I did ask him, but he cut me right off.''

Standing beside her husband, Meg rocked Matthew in her arms as the baby dozed off. ''He's a bit of a mystery man, isn't he!'' She watched as Mallory rolled her bikini into her towel. ''I must say I liked him, though. And that surprised me, after the way he's behaved.''

"He may have had a very good reason for his absence." Sam shot out a hand and batted back Andy's red-and-white vinyl beach ball as his son lobbed it over to him.

Mallory gave a derisive snort. "I don't think so. I already told you he went off with a woman."

"She must have been some woman, to divert him at a time like that." Sam slanted a mischievous glance at his wife. "The things some men will do for love!"

"Lust, more like!" said Mallory. "In the short time he's been here, Jordan Caine has made it clear that love isn't on his agenda."

"Too bad," said Meg with an impish grin. "The two of you looked good together!"

"My wife the matchmaker." Sam swatted Meg's bottom with his shirt before swinging the shirt on. "Watch out, Mallory. She'll have you at the altar before you know it."

"It's just that I'm so happy," Meg protested, "I want everybody else to be! But it's really too bad he's leaving tomorrow—for Matthew's sake," she added hurriedly as she saw the warning glint in Mallory's eyes.

"They can't be in the same room together—" Mallory glanced at her watch
"—because Matthew freaks out when he sees
Jordan's beard!" She got to her feet. "I really
should be getting back. It's after five…"

Andy threw the ball to her and as an unexpected gust of wind blew it sideways, she ran
a few steps in an attempt to catch it, but she
tripped and fell forward onto the sand, landing
on her hands and knees. Her quick laugh
changed to a gasp as she felt a sharp pain in
her left hand.

"Mallory…what's wrong?"

Meg's shadow fell over her as she sat back
and inspected her hand. She felt a wave of diz-
ziness when she saw the blood spurting from
the fleshy part of her palm. "I've cut myself!"

"Let me see." Sam's tone was as sharp as
whatever it was that had slashed her. He
crouched down beside her. "Damn, it's bad!
Meg, throw me a towel!"

Meg whisked a clean diaper from the baby's
diaper bag and thrust it at him. He pressed it
against Mallory's hand.

"Hold that there. Press it as *hard* as you
can." He hauled her to her feet. "Meg, can

you look after the baby? Andy'll help. I'll take Mallory to the clinic.'' He put an arm around her waist.

''It was a broken bottle.'' Andy's voice floated after them as they hurried up the beach. ''Look, Mom...''

Mallory didn't want to see it. She felt queasy. And thankful for Sam's support as they made for the Inn's parking lot, where he bundled her into his car.

''How're you doing?'' he asked as he threw himself down into the driver's seat and set the car into motion.

''Fine.'' But she swiftly withdrew her gaze from the wadded diaper when she saw that the blood was seeping through.

Swallowing a whimper, she slumped back in her seat and closed her eyes. But even when all she could see was black, the world still seemed to be tilting on its axis.

Jordan wasn't concerned when Mallory didn't come home by five. And wasn't concerned when she still hadn't come home at six. He was feeling peckish, though, so he made himself a hefty peanut-butter-and-jam sandwich, and washed it down with a glass of the leftover white wine.

When she hadn't turned up by seven, he shrugged, figuring she was having a good time and had stayed to enjoy the company. It was obvious the woman was a gregarious creature—unlike himself, who didn't care for crowds.

Didn't care for crowds, didn't care for small towns, didn't care for babies...and didn't care for redheads!

Although Mallory Madison was one redhead who might make him change his mind about that. If he were to hang around here long enough, which, of course, he wasn't about to do.

Not that he would ever go back to Zlobovia. But just thinking about that hellhole where he'd spent the past eight months in captivity plunged him into a deep depression.

With his thoughts in a turmoil, he prowled the house restlessly for a good half hour, ending up in the sitting room. His mood still dark, he sat in an armchair, staring into space as memories, bad memories, pressed in on him...

As he struggled to cope with them, he wondered—as he so often did—which had been worse: the mental torture inflicted by his captors; or the emotional anguish resulting from Janine's death and being unable to attend her funeral.

When the doorbell chimed, it startled him so that he jumped. Pulse hammering, he blinked back to the present. Rising stiffly, he walked to the window.

And saw a black Infiniti in the drive.

Who the hell…?

Frowning, he turned from the window, and made his way out to the front hall. As he did, he heard the click of the door opening. Mallory? Had to be her…who else would come in uninvited! But dammit, who had she brought home? He'd told her before she left that he wasn't in the mood for company. He'd meant it then, he meant it even more now.

The front door opened and two people appeared.

Meg's husband Sam…and Mallory. She was slumped against Sam, her face as white as the sling supporting her bandaged left hand. Her eyes were heavy, the lids drifting closed. Jordan stared at her in alarm.

She looked as if she was on the verge of collapse.

CHAPTER SIX

MALLORY felt as woozy as if she were stumbling through a cloud of cotton wool. Vaguely she heard Jordan ask, ''What the hell happened?'' And vaguely she heard Sam's reply.

''Bad cut…stitches…sedative…''

Jordan's response. ''Let's get her to bed…''

She barely managed to remain upright as they walked her to her room. She couldn't wait to lie down; couldn't wait to close her eyes and fade into oblivion.

Jordan asked, ''Where's the kid?''

She *hated* when he referred to Matthew that way. And before he left, she fully intended to tell him so!

''He's at the inn.'' Sam switched on the bedroom light, dispelling the lurking shadows. ''Meg's looking after him.''

He guided her over to the bed and sat her down on the edge of the mattress. ''Mallory.'' His insistent tone was designed to penetrate her fog. ''Where's your nightie?''

She tilted her chin. "I can manage now, thank you!" She tried to get up, but her head spun and with a frustrated mutter, she sank back onto the edge of the bed.

Jordan said, "I'll check the dresser..."

Mallory squinted up at him. "Thank you—" her voice came out sounding slurred "—but I haven't unpacked any of my clothes. I'll sleep in my undies. Now if you'll both just leave, I'll take off my dress and get into bed."

Jordan looked doubtful. "You'll never get out of that by yourself—not with one hand."

"Just open the back zipper for me." Ungainly as a puppet, she unlooped her sling. "I can do the rest."

Jordan stepped over to the bed, and she leaned forward. He swept aside her hair so he could find the zipper tab. He pulled the tab carefully down to the end. She felt his fingers brush her spine, every inch of the way. Even in her state of advanced stupor, she felt a shiver of reaction. This man generated more electricity than a hydro plant!

"I'll be back in a few minutes," he said, "to check that you haven't got yourself twisted into a knot."

"Bye, Mallory." Sam touched her shoulder. "Take care. Meg'll phone in the morning. Then we'll go from there."

After they'd left the room, Mallory wormed her way out of her dress and clambered awkwardly into bed.

The door was ajar, and as her eyes drifted shut, she could hear the rumble of deep male voices from the hall.

She wondered what they were saying, these two men who were so different: Sam Grainger, a man to whom home and hearth were everything; Jordan Caine, a man whose home was wherever he hung his hat...

And, he had told her, he never wore a hat!

Within minutes she was asleep. And in her sleep she was to dream of a dark-bearded nomad, destined to wander forever—alone and bareheaded!—over the face of the earth.

"Mallory's hand's going to be out of commission for at least a week." Sam stood on the front door stoop with Jordan. "But the first thing she said after the doc fixed her up was that she wanted the baby at home with her."

"Well, that's going to present a problem!"

"At least I persuaded her to leave Matthew at the inn, for tonight. But when she gets him home, she's going to need someone around full-timc. She won't be able to lift him or change him, and since she'll have to keep her hand out of water, she certainly won't be able to bathe him. Normally, Meg would pitch in, but she's under doctor's orders to take it easy. Elsa Carradine might help out—she's been baby-sitting Matthew during the week—"

"Mallory filled me in on Elsa." Jordan looked up at the white-paper moon in the darkening sky. "She won't be available—apparently she has family coming to stay over."

"Oh, right. James and Dee." Sam rubbed a weary hand over his nape. "Well, maybe Meg will come up with something tomorrow. In the meantime, you'll keep an eye on Mallory overnight? That hand's going to throb like hell when the painkiller wears off. The doc prescribed pills, they're in her bag—"

"Don't worry. I'll look out for her."

Sam gave a wry grin. "We didn't formally introduce ourselves." He stuck out his hand. "Sam Grainger."

"Jordan Caine." They shook hands firmly.

And then Sam said, "Too bad you have to leave tomorrow. There's a lot of work involved in looking after a baby—and Mallory badly needs a break. These past months have been tough on her—she's run herself ragged, driving here every weekend."

"How come she didn't make the move sooner?"

"She didn't want to give up her job in Seattle till she'd built up an emergency fund—she knew she needed to have a cushion. Mallory's very organized. But then, she's had to be, hasn't she—she's been a caregiver most of her life. It's high time somebody looked after her, for a change—but she's just so bloody independent!"

After Sam had driven away, Jordan stood for several long minutes, lost in thought, gazing out over the ocean. Then with an abrupt squaring of his shoulders, he turned on his heel and walked back into the house.

Mallory was already asleep when he returned to her room.

He paused in the doorway.

She lay flat on her back, her bandaged hand on her pillow. She had pulled the sheet up but the rise of her breasts was still visible—as were the narrow straps of her mocha bra, and the dainty lacy trim adorning the cups.

He felt a tug of desire.

Unwanted desire.

Cursing under his breath, he loped across the room to where Sam had dropped her bag, and swinging it up, took it to the kitchen. He found the pill bottle and carried it, along with a glass of water, back to the bedroom.

He switched off the wall light and in the moonrays streaming in through the uncurtained window, he tiptoed to the bedside table, where he deposited pill bottle and glass.

His next move was to sweep up the rocking chair and carry it to the darkest corner of the bedroom.

Then after taking off his shoes, he sprawled down onto the chair, stuck out his long legs, closed his tired eyes, and shutting all thoughts of Mallory Madison from his mind, willed himself to go to sleep.

He woke to the sound of a moan.

It had him shooting up out of his chair with

a clatter, his heart in his mouth, his eyes skidding around the dawn-grayed room.

It took fully seven seconds for him to remember where he was. And to accept that he was safe.

His breath shuddered out. His heart sank slowly back into its accustomed place.

''Jordan?'' Mallory's voice was rusty…and confused.

He raked his fingers through his hair as he crossed to the bed. Reaching out to flick on the bedside lamp, he said, ''Morning. How's it going?''

She grimaced. ''My hand feels as if it's been under a steamroller.''

''Time for a pain pill.''

''The bottle's in my—''

''I have it.'' He opened the bottle, spilled out a pill.

She levered herself up and supported herself on her right elbow. The movement had pushed down her sheet, and before she drew it up again, he caught a glimpse of rounded breasts straining against the confinement of a low-cut bra.

A tantalizing glimpse.

A glimpse that aroused him. *Painfully* aroused him.

As he handed her the pill, he was tempted to down one himself. Perhaps he had even more need of it than she did, he mused as he held out the water glass!

She tossed back the pill, chased it with a gulp of water. "Thanks." She returned the glass and slid down again onto her pillow.

"You're welcome." With an effort he switched his thoughts to a non-sexual track as he noticed how drawn she looked. "Can I get you something? Coffee? Toast?"

"I wouldn't mind a cup of tea—with a dash of milk." Her eyes were fixed on him unblinkingly, trusting and curious as the eyes of a child. "Why were you here, in my room, when I woke up?"

"I slept in the rocking chair."

Her gaze widened. And then he saw a faint flush colour her pale cheeks. "To watch over me?"

"Yeah." He grinned. "Guardian angel."

Her mouth curved in a smile. "You don't look like an angel," she said softly. "Not with that black beard."

She was beautiful. Despite her tangled hair and her unwashed face, she was beautiful. And as she looked up at him with amusement warming her lovely brown eyes, he had the oddest sensation that the floor had turned to quicksand.

It wasn't the first time, by any means, that he'd spent the night in a woman's bedroom…but it was the first time he'd done nothing but sleep…and the first time he'd still been there when dawn broke.

And it sure as *hell* was the first time he'd felt this bone-deep tenderness the morning after!

Warning bells buzzed in his head—warning bells he was not about to ignore. The last thing he wanted was to become emotionally involved with this woman.

He drew down his brow in a dark frown, in an attempt to appear as ferocious as she'd told Meg he was—but his act turned out to be in vain. She had already closed her eyes.

''So.'' He cleared his throat. ''Tea with a dash of milk coming up.''

He walked from the room but as he reached the hall, he was hit by a powerful and panicky urge to break into a run. An urge he somehow managed to resist.

Still, he felt as if he were fleeing.

From her, of course. And that would have been easy.

But fleeing from his emotions?

He knew only too well that that was impossible.

Mallory paid a visit to the bathroom while Jordan was gone and by the time he returned she was back in bed again, her face washed, her hair brushed. But she didn't hear him approach and so she was sniffing, and dabbing her eyes with a tissue, when he came in.

"What's wrong?" He walked over and set her mug of tea on the bedside table. "Pill not working yet?"

She heaved out a shaky sigh. "It's not that—the pill's working just fine. I'm feeling woozy already."

"Then what?"

She gave another sniff and tucked the tissue under her pillow. "I've only just realized how difficult it's going to be, looking after

Matthew. How on earth am I going to manage him, when I can't even put my hand in water!''

He offered the mug. ''You'll work something out.''

''Elsa's going to be too busy to help,'' she said as she took the mug, ''with James and Dee visiting.'' In a fretty tone she went on, ''And I can't ask Meg to help because she's under doctor's orders to take it easy—and so where am I going to find somebody I can trust to look after Matthew?''

Jordan felt a pang of concern as he noticed the dark shadows under her eyes and the pallor of her skin. ''Sam said Meg would surely come up with somebody to help you—''

''I'm not about to let just *anybody* care for him!'' She glared at him indignantly. ''It's not easy, looking after a baby. Take his bath, for instance—he's such a slippery customer, worse than an eel—he could drown in an *instant* if he wasn't held properly...and there's an art in that, believe me! *Then,* when he's crawling *about,* he picks up every little thing and pokes it into his mouth and if somebody wasn't watching him every *second,* he could choke to death before—''

"Enough!"

She looked startled.

"Listen." He tried to sound reassuring. "Worrying never solved anything. Drink your tea, and get back to sleep for a while. Hey, here's a thought. What about those women Elsa chatted about when she was here yesterday?"

"Women?"

"When you were feeding Matthew, she said something about her boarders popping over sometime to pay a visit. Would they be available to—"

Her laugh had a hysterical edge. "The three sisters? Angelina, Monique and Emily? Jordan, they're all in their *eighties!* They dote on Matthew but I wouldn't dream of letting them bathe him or—"

"Okay, the three elderly sisters are out." He suppressed an impatient sigh. Surely Mallory was exaggerating the difficulty of this situation. Seashore wasn't exactly a bustling metropolis, but there must be *one* competent woman out there who could spare a few days to baby-sit...especially with the financial compensation he was prepared to offer. "But you're to stop worrying your pretty little head over—''

''Don't talk down to me, Jordan!'' Annoyance sparked from eyes that were becoming drowsy. She took a noisy sip of her tea and gulped it down. Gulped down some more, till the mug was empty, before she glared up at him again. ''You don't have one clue how hard it is to look after a baby!''

''How hard can it be?'' he drawled. ''You just put food in at one end and tidy up at the other. Walk him regularly and when he wants to play, toss him a toy.'' He grinned. ''Much like looking after a puppy.''

Her mouth gaped open. ''A *puppy?*'' She stared at him, her expression incredulous. ''You think looking after a baby's like looking after a *puppy?*'' She thrust the empty mug at him and shot him the kind of disgusted look she might have given a dead rat. ''Here!'' she snapped. ''Take this and get out. It's no wonder Matthew took an instant dislike to you— he may be just nine months old, but he sure had you taped!''

''But I—''

''Out!''

He'd only been trying to calm her down...but obviously he'd said the wrong thing. Okay, groveling was called for here. ''Well, I guess,'' he started in an apologetic tone, ''there's more to it than what I just said. With a baby, you have to dress them and wash their clothes and—''

She jerked around onto her stomach, buried her face in her pillow and jammed her right hand over her right ear.

He got the message.

Heaving out a perplexed sigh, he turned and headed for the door. She was being unreasonable...but he had to make allowances. She had a mighty sore hand and that was maybe making her fractious.

When she felt better, they'd talk again. He'd make her see sense.

He closed the door quietly and leaned for a moment against it, wondering how he'd got himself into this mess.

He was just about to move away, when he heard a sound from the bedroom. He cocked his head and listened. And as the sound came again, he slumped. She was sobbing. Softly sobbing.

Oh, dammit to hell! She was crying again! And when this particular woman wept, it snuck in and touched a part of him that he kept determinedly barricaded...

He knew he should go back in and try to comfort her. But he just stood there, feeling torn in two. Stood there, leaning back against the door, till the sound eventually faded.

It took a long time.

And he guessed she had cried herself to sleep.

Feeling rotten, and useless, and guilty, he went through to the kitchen and was irritably sticking her empty mug in the dishwasher when the phone rang.

He leaped to answer it before the sound could waken her.

The caller was Sam.

"We have a problem," the hotelier said without preamble. "Meg's having contractions—they're mild, but the doc's told me to bring her over to the clinic so he can check her out. I need to drop Matthew off—can you cope?"

Jordan had been staring with unfocused eyes at the chrome kettle on the counter. But when

he heard Sam say, "Can you cope?" he focused his gaze sharply...and found himself
staring at his reflection in the shiny chrome. A
distorted reflection of his face and his stubby
black beard. The beard that had sent Matthew
into a hysterical fit on the two occasions when
he'd seen it.

"Jordan?" Sam's voice was urgent. "Are
you there?"

Jordan jerked his thoughts into order. "I'm
here."

"You'll be okay with the baby?"

Jordan felt his heart thud six times before
he answered. "Yeah. I'll be okay with the
baby."

"Fine. We'll see you in about ten minutes."

"Mallory's asleep. I'll wait for you out
front, so you don't have to ring the doorbell."

As Jordan put the phone down, his lips
twisted in an ironic smile. He was trapped,
well and truly trapped, and he knew it. Twelve
more hours and he'd have been out of here...if
things had gone according to plan.

But then, as he'd so often found in the past,
things rarely did.

*   *   *

The morning was bright and breezy, the sky pale and streaked with fading brush-strokes of pink.

Jordan felt the warm wind lift his hair as he walked to the end of the drive. Looking along Seaside Lane, he saw Sam's black Infiniti skimming towards him.

The car drew to a halt by the curb, and Sam got out.

"Hi, there," he greeted Jordan. "Sorry about the short notice." He opened the trunk and while he hauled out Matthew's stroller, Jordan leaned into the car at the driver's side to say hello to Meg.

"Hi, Jordan." She was cuddling the baby, who was asleep, and cosily dressed in a blue terry sleeper. "He's been fed and changed, so he should doze for a couple of hours or so if you can keep the house quiet."

"How're *you* doing?" Jordan asked.

She wrinkled her nose. "It's a false alarm, I'm sure. How's Mallory?"

"She had a good night. Didn't waken till half an hour ago. Then she took a painkiller and went back to sleep."

Sam opened the passenger door and after scooping up the baby, settled him in the stroller.

"You'll be fine with Matthew," Meg said. "Don't look so worried, Jordan! Babies survive not *because* of you, but in *spite* of you! And once Mallory's awake she'll tell you what to do. Meantime, if you do have to lift him, just remember to support his head. That's really important."

"Right. Support his head." Jordan stepped back to let Sam get into the driver's seat.

"Give Mallory our love," Meg called.

A moment later the car was whizzing away down the road.

Meg sat back in her seat, a smug smile on her face. "He shaved off his beard, Sam. That's a good sign."

Sam glanced at her. "What do you mean, a good sign?"

"It means," she said contentedly, "that he's caring enough that he didn't want to upset the baby. And he wouldn't have shaved it off unless he was planning to stay a while. Which is what I hoped."

"But surely it's not necessary for him to stay on? Last night, when your friend Sally came over to bathe Matthew and put him to bed, didn't she offer to help Mallory out? She was a maternity nurse, she'd be perfect for—"

"You didn't see them together."

"Who? Sally and—"

"No, sweetheart. *Jordan and Mallory.* Sam, the sparks between those two—well, just let me say this. When you came back to Seashore for Dee's wedding and Elsa saw us together, she said she knew right away that we'd end up at the altar. She saw the sparks."

Sam took in a deep breath. "Meg, are you telling me that you engineered this whole thing so that—"

"Sam, how could you ever suggest such a thing!" She looked at him indignantly, but when he saw the mischievous twinkle in her eyes, he groaned.

"Sweetheart, what about those contractions?"

"Oh—" she made an airy gesture "—I did have a few faint flutterings...of course, it may turn out to have been indigestion...but we shouldn't take any chances, should we!"

Laughing as she heard Sam mutter ominously about the dire things that could happen to matchmakers in general—and to his own beautiful matchmaker in particular!—she adjusted the rearview mirror so she could look back. She was just in time to see Jordan before he disappeared from view.

He was wheeling the stroller up the drive.

And he couldn't have looked more apprehensive if the stroller had been packed with dynamite.

Jordan rolled the stroller into the sitting room and parked it by the window.

"Stay there," he whispered. "I'm going to make some coffee but I'll be right back."

His nephew's lips parted slightly and he issued a faint snoring sound. About to move away, Jordan paused.

It was the first time he'd had a good chance to look at Janine's baby—on the two previous occasions when they'd met, the kid had screamed his guts out. Now he found himself drawn to stand there and gaze curiously at him.

He'd looked at babies before—in passing, and without any interest. They'd all looked much the same to him, with their round little faces and tiny squashed features—the only thing distinguishing one from the other being their hair. Some had none at all; some had fly-away brown wisps; while others had thatches so black and thick they seemed better suited to a Sumo wrestler than an infant…

This kid's hair was blond. Smooth and glossy. And his features weren't squashed; they were perfect—a miniature version of his mother's.

He was a nice-looking tyke.

And asleep. That was the main thing. Asleep…for now.

Jordan turned on his heel and made for the kitchen. But while he waited for the coffee to drip, his nerves were tensed, alert to any cry from the sitting room.

It was with a deep sense of relief that he found the baby still asleep when he returned with his coffee, along with a crisp copy of the morning paper which had been flung against the front door as he passed.

He set his mug on a side table, sank onto the armchair beside it, spread out the paper, and settled down to read.

*   *   *

He'd reached the last page of the financial section when he heard the steady hum of water in the pipes.

But even as he thought ''Good, Mallory's up!'' he heard an ominous whimper from across the room.

He rose and tentatively tiptoed to the stroller.

The baby was still lying on his back...but his eyes were squinched open and fixed on the ceiling. His face was red, his mouth turned down, the lower lip quivering. Jordan had no experience of babies, but he sensed that this one was about to embark on a major crying jag.

He rubbed a hand over his jaw, thankful he'd gone to the trouble of shaving off his beard after Sam phoned. It now remained to be seen if his nephew had screamed because of the black stubble...or just for the sheer hell of it!

He stepped forward. Setting his hands loosely on his hips, he cleared his throat.

''Hi, kid,'' he said in a conversational tone. ''What's up?''

The baby jerked its attention from the ceiling, his gray eyes wide and startled as they fixed on his uncle. For a long, endlessly long moment, he just looked up at Jordan, scrutinizing him, weighing him up, wondering...

Jordan was about to growl, "So, kid, what are you seeing?" when slowly, very slowly, a smile crept over Matthew's face...and he reached up his arms.

He didn't say "up"; couldn't say "up." But Jordan knew damned well that he wanted up!

He'd never touched a baby before, far less lifted one. And he had no intention of lifting this one...

But when the smile gradually faded, to be replaced again by an expression of distress, the beginning of a wail, Jordan said hurriedly, "Okay, okay, you win!"

He wiped his palms on the seat of his jeans. What was it Meg had said? If you have to lift him, support his head. Or was it his neck? Oh, rats, he'd support both!

Drawing in a taut breath, he leaned over, and sliding his hands around the little body, he raised him, as carefully as if he were made of glass.

The kid was heavier, much more solidly built, than he looked. And wriggly. Dammit, he was wriggly! Catching hold of him just before he leaped like a fish from his hands, he somehow managed to tuck him into the crook of his arm…supporting neck, head and everything else as he did so.

''Gotcha, you little monster!''

Chuckling, Matthew grabbed his shirt and tried to stuff it into his mouth. Afraid he might catch the button, Jordan tugged it from his fingers and Matthew gooed happily at him.

Smiled right up at him. As though they were sharing a wonderful private joke together.

Man to man.

Jordan felt a huge lump rise in his throat, a lump that threatened to choke him. Tears pricked his eyes as he struggled to gather himself together. What the hell was happening here? He'd never in his life felt this way before…

Completely undone.

And by a baby's smile.

He was still reeling from the shock of it when he heard the door open behind him.

CHAPTER SEVEN

TO THE manner born.

The phrase hurtled into Mallory's mind as she stared at Jordan and the baby held so tenderly in the crook of his arm. With his ink-black hair and clean-shaven jaw, his crisp white shirt and hip-hugging blue jeans, he could have been posing for the cover of *Perfect Parent* magazine....

Except that this was no pose. The tenderness in his expression was real.

As was the delighted "Hey, I've found a best buddy!" expression on Matthew's cherubic face.

These two, she realized with a surge of panic, were made for each other. While *she* had slept, *they* had bonded.

And that could throw a spanner into her well-oiled plans....

Jordan had turned to look at her. His eyes were dazed. It was obvious that this fledgling affinity to his nephew was as startling to him as it was to her.

Crushing back her dismay, she walked over to him.

"I see," she said, "that you've made friends."

A grin inched over his face as he looked at Matthew. "Yeah. He's a cute little tyke, no two ways about it."

She *itched* to snatch the baby from him. But with one hand? Hardly. "Thank you for keeping an eye on him."

"Meg dropped him off on her way to the clinic."

"Yes, I called her just now—she filled me in."

"Is she home already?"

"Mmm. She told me it was a false alarm."

"That's good."

Meg had also told her she hadn't yet come up with anyone to help out with Matthew.

"That was quite a sigh." Jordan looked at her questioningly. "What's on your mind?"

"Oh. It's just...I still don't have anyone to help me with Matthew once you leave today."

"I'm staying."

Her brown eyes widened. "Excuse me?"

"I'll stay. Till your hand's functional again."

She looked stunned. "But…"

"But what?"

"I thought you were in a rush to leave town."

"I can spare a week or two."

"But you *hate* small towns!"

His laugh was dry. "I'll survive."

"But you know nothing about babies!"

"During the day, you can show me. And I'll put Matthew's crib upstairs in his room so I can hear him through the night if he cries."

"But you won't know what to do if he does!"

"You'll move upstairs too. We'll both hear him…then we can rendezvous in his room and you can keep me on the right track. Are you okay with that?"

As okay as she'd feel about an invitation to rendezvous in a dark forest with a panther! But what choice did she have? "I don't really have any alternative, do I?"

"Then that's settled." He frowned. And looked down at Matthew. "Something," he said in an ominous tone, "feels warm and wet."

The baby looked up at him with an innocent "Who, me?" expression.

Mallory headed for the door. "Follow me," she said. "It's time to get you started on Baby-minding 101."

As Jordan changed Matthew's diaper, Mallory was so nervous her heart took up temporary lodging in her mouth.

But looking back on the episode after, she found herself chuckling at the memory of strong lean hands trying awkwardly to cope with a small wriggly body—a body that seemed determined to launch itself from the changing table…and equally determined to thwart every repeated attempt to tuck the snow-white cotton diaper into place.

One thing she knew for certain: she'd never forget the startled look on Jordan's face when Matthew suddenly and unconcernedly issued a perfect arc that lightly sprinkled the front of his dismayed uncle's shirt.

But Jordan, give him his due, had battled on to the end. And though the diaper finished up askew and he'd pricked himself twice, she assured him that for a first attempt, he'd done very well indeed.

"However," she added, as he put Matthew into his crib, "to make things easier for you, I'll buy some disposables."

He started unbuttoning his shirt. "Disposable whats?" He raised an eyebrow and looked at her curiously.

Oh, boy, she thought, did this surrogate dad ever have a lot to learn! "Diapers."

His shirt fell open and she was treated to the sight of his lean muscled chest with its smattering of crisp black hair. Her nerve endings shot to vibrant life, waving wildly to get her attention but she snatched her gaze up and focused it determinedly on his face. "Disposables stick together with tape—you don't need to use safety pins."

"You're kidding!" He sounded astonished. "What the heck will they think of next!" Peeling off his shirt, he made for the door.

Mallory's traitorous gaze flew to his naked back—to his powerful shoulders, his tanned skin, his hard muscles—and clung there.

"Come right down again after you've changed," she called after him...

Then horrified that her words had come out as a sultry invitation, she cleared her throat and added in a sharp authoritarian tone, "It's time for Matthew's snack—I'll need you to carry him to the kitchen."

She slumped as she heard him bound up the stairs. She'd never before been exposed to such raw male magnetism—and it left her weak at the knees. But ignoring the wobbly sensation, she retrieved Matthew's wet diaper from the changing table and took it through to the laundry room. She spent a few minutes there before returning to the bedroom.

Matthew was gurgling happily in his crib. Leaning over the side, she plucked up his rattle.

"You like him," she said, "don't you!" She pointed the rattle at him accusingly, just out of his reach. "Now that he doesn't have that black beard."

Matthew lunged at the rattle and with a laugh she let him have it. But even as she did, her thoughts remained with his uncle.

Jordan Caine, she decided helplessly, was far too attractive for his own good. And for hers. With the beard he'd looked rakish. Without it, he looked...kissable.

She stifled a groan and said to the baby. "Your uncle's a hunk. It's no wonder you fell for him. And if I don't watch out, I'll be doing the same thing myself. It's a very real danger—"

"What's a very real danger?"

She gasped. Whirling around, she saw that Jordan had come into the room and was only a few feet away. He'd changed into a black T-shirt.

"There's a very real danger," she said, grabbing at the first thing to come into her head, "that if you creep up on me like that, you'll give me a heart attack."

"You want me to wear a bell around my neck?" His grin was wicked. "Makes sense," he drawled. "After all, I *am* a pussycat!"

His smile melted her. And that infuriated her. She simply must not let this man steal his way into her affections. Ignoring his provocative comment, she said, "Would you take Matthew to the kitchen for me?"

"Sure."

She stood back and watched as he bent over the crib.

"Careful!" she said. "Support his—"

"Yeah." He slid his hand under the baby's head and neck. "I know. Meg told me it was very important."

He was looking down at Matthew as he spoke, and his face creased in a lopsided smile. A smile that caused the baby to chuckle...and Mallory's heart to ache.

Ache for what, she wasn't sure. But she felt a deep yearning for *something*...something that was missing in her life. Was it the same "something" that Jordan and Matthew had so miraculously found in each other?

Maybe what she had never found was a kindred spirit. She and Nick had lived together in close accord...but his work had always come first and he'd been wrapped up in it.

He'd never been wrapped up in her. Not the way that Jordan and the baby were wrapped up in each other—

"Ready?"

She jerked her thoughts into order as Jordan spoke.

"Ready," she said, and led the way to the kitchen.

"What'll he have for his snack?" he asked.

"Juice and toast." She opened the fridge and took out the juice jug. "If you put him into his chair, I'll feed him." Taking a lidded plastic cup from the cupboard, she set it on the island, before popping a slice of whole-wheat bread into the toaster.

"You can manage?" Jordan slid the baby into his chair.

"Yes—" The doorbell chimed and Mallory said, "Oh, that'll be the sisters. I phoned them after I talked with Meg, and invited them over for a visit with Matthew. Keep an eye on him, while I get the door?"

Without waiting for an answer, she took off.

Jordan scowled. "The sisters," he said to Matthew. "How can you stand it, all these women fussing over you? I'm outta here, buddy, the minute your auntie comes back."

Matthew reached up to catch a mote of dust. "Ma...ma!"

"Mama?" Jordan shrugged. "Okay... whatever you want to call her. But to me, she's just the nanny!"

He was whisking the toast from the toaster when Mallory brought her visitors into the kitchen.

She introduced them and as he shook their hands in turn, he swiftly summed them up. Angelina—gray-haired and grimly disapproving—was the leader. Monique—fair-haired and clinging—was her follower. And Emily—tiny pink-haired Emily, peeking cautiously at him over top of half glasses—was the peacemaker.

"Well, ladies," he said mildly, "I guess since you've come to visit Matthew, I'll leave and—"

"You're good at that, aren't you!" With a disdainful sniff, Angelina pulled out a chair and sat down, her back rigid as a career soldier's.

Monique sidled over to the next chair and bonelessly slid onto it. "Oh, yes, Angelina." She sighed. "He is!"

"But he did come back!" Emily would have remained standing but an embarrassed-looking Mallory pulled out a chair for her. She perched on the edge of the seat and looked eagerly at Jordan. "You did come back, didn't you?"

Unbelievable. The attack; the backup; the call for a cease-fire. It was all he could do not to laugh out loud.

But Emily was sweet and he didn't want to hurt her. "Oh, yeah." He directed his response to her. "I'm back."

"And he's going to stay on, till my hand is better," Mallory said.

"Well, it's high *time,*" Angelina said tartly, "that you pulled your weight around here, Mr. Caine."

"Oh, it is!" whispered Monique. "It really is!"

Mallory's cheeks were scarlet. She began to murmur something, but he interrupted her. "You're right, ladies," he said placatingly. "And I intend to do just that."

Emily patted her fluffy pink hair. "I know you'll do just fine, Mr. Caine. You have a nice face. A very *good* face." She glanced up at Mallory. "Don't you think so, dear? Don't you agree that Mr. Caine has a very good face?"

Jordan managed to keep his Very Good Face straight as Mallory cocked her head to

one side and made a big production of inspect-
ing it. Her cheeks were still flushed but her
eyes had a naughty twinkle. "Well—" she
supported her chin with the tip of her index
finger as she scrutinized him "—perhaps those
black eyelashes are too long and luxuriant for
a man; and perhaps the nose, though strong, is
a bit off-kilter; and the lower lip…" She grimaced. "I'm being picky here, but it *is* rather
too full to be classic. I guess you're right,
though, Emily." He could see she was having
a merry old time at his expense. "Despite
those flaws, as faces go, this one really isn't
too bad."

Impudent wench!

But before he could come up with a suitably
impudent response, he heard a rat-tat on the
outside kitchen door.

"I'll get that." As he spoke, he was already
on his way to the door. What a blessed opportunity to escape! Whoever this was, he'd let
the person in and then be off himself like a
shot.

He snatched the door open…and stopped
short. There on the stoop stood Dr. Tyler Scott,
owner of a yacht, possessor of a fortune.

Sleekly dressed in a charcoal suit, an onyx-and-gray silk tie, and a dove-gray shirt, the man had an anticipatory smile on his face—a face, Jordan noted sourly, that had standard male eyelashes, a ruler-straight nose, and lips chiseled to the point of absolute perfection.

Classic didn't even begin to describe the good doctor's looks—and to add to the *charming* picture, he was carrying a precious little bouquet of purple and yellow pansies.

Norman Rockwell, eat your heart out!

"Who is it?" Mallory called.

The doctor flashed Jordan a Hollywood smile before bypassing him. "It's me, Mallory." The voice was rich—well, of course it would be, wouldn't it! "Just dropped by to see how my patient's doing today."

Jordan leaned wearily against the doorjamb, his back to the room, as Mallory exclaimed, "Oh, Tyler, these are beautiful—I just *love* pansies! Come away in, I'm just about to put on a pot of coffee."

No sooner had she spoken than Angelina said warmly, "Dr. Scott. What a delightful surprise!"

Then Monique. "Oh, yes, Angelina. Indeed it is!"

Emily said, "Have you met Mr. Caine, Dr. Scott?"

But by that time, Jordan had pushed himself from the doorjamb and slipped outside. As he closed the door behind him, he heard Emily say, "Oh, what a pity! He's gone..."

When he passed the kitchen window, he heard everyone fussing over the baby. The babble set his temples throbbing. Thank the Lord he'd been given a chance to get out of there....

But Ms. Madison seemed to be in her element. How could she *stand* having all these people around!

He opened the side gate and as he closed it he heard voices coming from his left. He glanced around and saw a couple standing on the Welcome mat at the front door. The man had a fingertip pressed to the doorbell.

Ye gods, more visitors! Rolling his eyes, Jordan marched over the road and down to the beach. If today was a typical day at Number Five Seaside Lane, the next couple of weeks were going to be a grind.

Especially if the perfect-faced and immac-ulately-dressed Dr. Scott turned out to be a regular visitor!

Scowling, Jordan dug his hands into his pockets, wheeled north, and tramped bad-temperedly towards town.

"Oh, hi there, I *thought* I heard you come in."

Jordan tossed his package into the hall closet and turned to glance at Mallory as she came out of the sitting room. She looked pale. And tired. Damn all these people, didn't they see she wasn't up to having so many visitors milling around?

But he limited himself to saying, "The house is quiet."

"Everybody left a few minutes ago. You just missed Elsa's son James and his wife Dee—Dee's Meg's sister. They arrived for a visit only moments after you took off."

"I saw them at the front door as I was leav-ing." He saw her eyebrows rise at sound of his crusty growl. With an effort he lightened his tone as he went on, "I wasn't in the mood for company. I went for a walk."

"I'm glad you're back."

"You are?" Why did that simple remark make his heart flip around like a trout in a net? She was not his type, he reminded himself irritably. But he had to admit that even with her arm in a sling, she was an eye-catching sight in that blue sundress with its low scoop neck—

"Mmm." Smiling ruefully, she nodded towards the bedroom. "Dee put Matthew down in his crib—but I was concerned that he might wake up again before you got back."

Oh. *That* was why she was glad to see him.

Well, good, he told himself firmly. What they had was a strictly practical arrangement; he didn't *want* her being glad to see him for any other reason. He certainly didn't want her getting any romantic ideas about him!

"You needn't have worried." He used a deliberately offhand tone. "I wasn't away too long and when I got back, I hung around on the beach, watching for your company to go. I wasn't about to leave you in the lurch."

"Thank you. I appreciate that."

"Those sisters—they're quite something, aren't they?"

"I'm sorry if they offended you. I did ask them, before they came around, to be...polite. But—"

"They spoke their mind. That doesn't bother me. I prefer that to having people pussyfooting around." He paused before going on coolly, "What *does* bother me is a lack of privacy. Do you spill out the minutiae of your everyday life to *all* your neighbours?"

She stiffened. "You consider your absence at your sister's funeral minutiae?"

"I consider it nobody's business but my own."

"Since you won't deign to explain your absence," she retorted, "then you can't expect others to understand—" She broke off and he saw a spasm of pain cross her face. Wincing, she cupped her good hand under the sling.

Dammit. "You look all in." He was as bad as those visitors—worse, actually. They hadn't upset her. "And it's no wonder, after the hectic pace you set yourself the past several months. You should go to bed for a while. Get some rest."

"I *hate* going to bed during the day."

"Then at least lie down in the sitting room. I'll keep an eye on Matthew—if he wakens, I'll lift him."

"But if he needs changing—"

"I'll manage. I bought a package of disposables. I can change him...and if necessary, I can give him juice, take him out for a walk in his stroller—whatever." He frowned at her as she looked dubious. "Trust me, Mallory. He'll come to no harm in my care."

She bit her lip. And then said, with a sigh, "All right. Thank you." She started towards the kitchen.

He grasped her right arm. "Where are you going?"

She turned big brown eyes up to him. "To get you my baby book—anything you need to know, including what he's allowed to eat— you'll find in there. Oh, and I've made up a batch of baby formula, the bottles are in the fridge." As she went on to tell him how to warm the milk to the right temperature, he found his attention wandering.

She was a temptation. He wanted to kiss those pouty lips, find out if they were as luscious as they looked. Wanted to run his fingers through her hair, find out if it was as silky as it seemed. Wanted to pull her body close, find out if it was as sweetly voluptuous as it promised— She'd finished talking.

He realized he was still holding her arm and he released it abruptly before his desires converted themselves into reality. "Okay, no problem. Now you go lie down."

"Don't hesitate to waken me if you need anything," she said, and turned away.

As she did, he barely managed to resist a politically incorrect urge to pat her sexy little bottom.

Dammit, he thought as he headed for the kitchen, he shouldn't have grasped her arm. That was a mistake. Once he'd touched her, he wanted to touch her again. And again. And again. Here, there...and every other erotic where.

Mallory slept for a couple of hours. When she woke, she went hunting for Jordan. She found him outside.

He'd set up one of the lawn chairs in the shade of the apple tree. He lay sprawled back comfortably in it, with Matthew dozing in his arms.

As she padded over the sunwarmed lawn in her bare feet, Jordan squinted up at her and examined her face.

"You look a bit better." He sounded satisfied. "Your face has some colour. How's the hand?"

"It's not so bad now. How has Matthew been?"

"He slept till around three. I've fed him—I gave him mashed banana and cereal, and a bottle of juice."

Mallory indicated the food smears on the front of Jordan's T-shirt. "A bit of a battle, was it?"

Jordan grinned. "He was determined to feed himself. So in the end, I gave him a spoon too, and it became a joint effort. Except that most of his ended up on the wall. Still, I got enough down him to stave off hunger pangs!"

She wished he wouldn't smile at her in that warmly intimate way. It played havoc with her senses and created a delicious little shiver that danced from nerve ending to nerve ending till it reached a twitchy sensitive spot deep inside her, where it pirouetted disturbingly.

She wrenched her thoughts from sex to laundry. ''I'll take the baby while you change your shirt.'' Sinking down on her knees, she manoeuvred herself into a cross-legged position and waited for Jordan to hand over the baby.

He got up from the lawn chair, and crouching down beside her, tucked Matthew into the crook of her arm. She was exposed to Jordan's disturbingly earthy male scent and she silently willed him to get out of her space.

He was in no hurry.

Stroking tanned fingers gently over the baby's head, he sent her a sideways glance. ''Fancy a pizza for dinner? I noticed a take-out place in town, next to the drugstore.''

''Oh, I can make something—''

''Uh-uh. You need a break. What toppings do you like?''

She could see he wasn't about to listen to any arguments. ''I like Hawaiian. But is that okay with you?''

''That's fine. I'll give them a call.''

At that, he did get up, and she breathed a sigh of relief.

"While you were asleep," he said, "I moved the crib upstairs. After dinner, I'll take your boxes up to your room and while you're unpacking I'll fix the fence." With that, he sauntered away towards the house.

She was tempted to watch him, because she did find his walk very sexy. Not a *swagger* exactly, but confident—without being arrogant.

She was proud of herself that instead of watching him, she managed to keep her attention focused on Matthew.

Which was, of course, where it belonged.

They ate pizza on the patio and Jordan drank a bottle of beer that had been in the fridge for months. He offered to share it but she said better not, because of her medication.

After they'd eaten, they fed the baby and then while Jordan carried her boxes upstairs, Mallory sat with Matthew and held him while he finished his bottle of formula.

Around seven-thirty, Jordan changed the baby's diaper and settled him in the crib, in his new room.

He stuck his thumb in his mouth and closed his eyes.

They went out and left the door ajar.

"I've opened your boxes," Jordan said as they paused in the passageway. "Give me a shout if you need any help. I'll be out in the backyard."

After he'd gone, she went into her bedroom and spent a couple of hours unpacking. By the time she was finished she felt tired and grubby. A soak in a hot bath, she decided, was called for.

Half an hour later, wearing her nightie and her yellow terry robe, she went downstairs. Jordan was still outside. She called to him from the back door, "Are you coming in?"

"I'll be a while yet."

"Would you like some hot chocolate?"

"No thanks."

"Good night, then," she said. "I'm going to bed now."

"See you in the morning," he said. And added, with a wry smile in his voice, "Unless there's a call in the night!"

The call came just before dawn.

Mallory had been in a deep sleep, but woke

abruptly as a cry pierced the early morning quiet. Pushing herself groggily up on her elbow, she was about to slide to her feet, when the sound came again. A sound so wild and harsh it chilled her blood.

It came from Jordan's room.

CHAPTER EIGHT

TERROR SLAMMED into Jordan.

Jolted from sleep, he lurched to a sitting position while his mind scrambled desperately back to reality.

Back from the nightmare.

Which was always the same.

As the thudding of his heart gradually decelerated, he whispered a hoarse oath. Then swiveling sideways, he sat on the edge of the bed, bare feet to the carpet, his head in his hands as memories pounded him without mercy...

Russian roulette. Or at least, he amended bitterly, Zlobovian roulette: the gun to his temple, the blindfolded eyes, the horror, the terror, the unspeakable dread.

The click.

He shuddered, the same way he'd shuddered then when he'd discovered that for that moment, he was still alive. But next time, would he be—

"Jordan?"

He jerked his head up as Mallory's voice came to him. For a moment, she was just a dark blur against the moonlight streaming in through the window. But as his eyes adjusted, he saw her more clearly. She was wearing a short nightie, her face was shadowed, her hair glowed like fire.

He expelled a harsh breath. "Go back to bed."

"But—"

"It's nothing. Just a bad dream." He clenched his hands and planted them on his knees. "It's over."

She hesitated. "Can I get you something?"

He needed what he was sure she wouldn't have. "Scotch."

"Okay…"

"You have some?" His eyes glinted.

"Janine and Tom had a house warming party—I remember hardly anybody drank Scotch, the bottle must still be around somewhere. I'll go look for it. How do you like it? With water? Ice? Or—"

"I'll come down." He pushed to his feet. Leaning over to the end of the bed, he grabbed his jeans, pulled them on.

"Your back," she murmured. "It's soaking wet. You'll get a chill." She plucked a towel from the top of his dresser and walked over to him. "Turn around."

He reached out a hand. "I can do that."

"Let me."

He hesitated, and then gave a "Why not!" shrug.

Fisting his hands on his hips, he turned his back to her, and stood, legs braced slightly apart. She rubbed his shoulders vigorously, then rubbed the towel over his ribs, down his spine...

He could hear her quick breathing, smell her sleepy scent. He found her closeness disturbing. Arousing. He wanted to turn and drag her body urgently against his, bury his face in that incredible cloud of glossy curls...

She finished with an energetic attack on the small of his back, rough as if she were scrubbing a cement doorstep.

"There," she said, "that should do it."

He turned and she was draping the towel over the bed rail. "Thanks," he said.

"You're welcome."

She walked towards the open doorway but as she reached it, she was caught in the light slanting from her bedroom across the way. It outlined her figure through hcr flimsy nightie—her tiny waist, curvy hips, long elegant legs...

Temptation. Irresistible temptation.

Flinging caution to the winds he strode after her, and caught up with her as she reached the passage. Clasping her right arm, he turned her to face him. "What's your hurry?"

She raised her eyebrows. "I'm going to get your Scotch. Isn't that what you want?"

"What I want," he murmured, "is to kiss you."

Her eyes took on a startled expression. "And do you always get what you want?" She tilted her chin haughtily.

"Usually I do," he drawled, "when the other person wants the same thing."

"I wasn't even *thinking* about kissing you!"

"Maybe not at this moment—but can you honestly say you've *never* thought about kissing me?"

"I've thought about it," she returned with an airy toss of her head. "After all, you're an attractive man and you have more than your fair share of charisma. But *thinking* about kissing you is a far cry from actually doing it!''

''Thinking about it is good.'' He snagged a loose auburn curl that had fallen forward. The texture, he found to his immense satisfaction, was just as silky as he'd guessed it would be. ''Doing it will be even better.''

''You're very sure of yourself!''

He'd never seen poutier lips—lips that gave a whole new dimension to the word *luscious*.

''Some things,'' he said lazily, ''a man just knows.''

''From experience, of course!''

He grinned. ''I'm no virgin. But then—'' the grin became a smirk ''—neither are you!''

''There's one big difference between the two of us. For you, a kiss is just a kiss. I, on the other hand, don't toss my kisses around lightly. Before I get to that stage with a man, I expect to at least have a close friendship with him. You and I are practically strangers!''

''Aren't you forgetting something?''

She fixed him with a cool gaze.

''The thunderbolt.'' He twirled the curl more tightly around his finger and used it to draw her face to his. "When the thunderbolt strikes, it annihilates reason."

Their lips were so close a sheet of paper could barely have passed between them. He felt the heat of her skin; heard the sharp catch of her breath. Her eyes had closed, her body tense with anticipation

And when she swayed against him, her breasts brushing his chest, he knew she was his for the taking.

But her very vulnerability jolted him back to sanity. If he were to take advantage of her now, he knew she would despise herself later. And probably despise him too.

Chasing after her had been a huge mistake.

And one he must rectify. Immediately.

Drawing on every vestige of his self-control, he kissed her lips lightly and swiftly, and then drew away from her.

She blinked...and he saw bewilderment in her eyes.

He faked a teasing smile. "That's all I wanted. Just a friendly kiss. Do you have a problem with that?"

"No." She swallowed hard. "No," she repeated, with a crack in her voice. "I don't have a problem with that."

"Good." Dammit, he'd upset her. He hated to do that. But in the end he'd have upset her a lot more if he hadn't put the brakes on. "Let's go downstairs now," he said conversationally, "and hunt up that bottle of Scotch."

She cleared her throat. "You go ahead. I'll…join you in a minute. I'm going to put on my robe."

Without waiting for a response, she fled into her room and shut the door behind her. Leaning against it weakly, she hissed out a shaky sigh.

She'd already acknowledged to herself that she liked Jordan. What she now admitted was that she had *wanted* him to kiss her. But not a friendly kiss. She'd wanted him to kiss her with the same kind of desperation she'd felt.

Not only kiss her, but take her into his bed.

And if she'd let him, wouldn't that have been the most foolish thing she'd ever done? Yes, she acknowledged, it would. But it would also have been the most wondrous.

And how could she be so sure of that? Well, to paraphrase Jordan Caine himself: Some things a woman just knows!

* * *

"I found the Scotch." Jordan was pouring himself a nip when Mallory came into the kitchen. "Are you going to join me?"

"Heavens, no!" She glanced at the microwave clock and yawned. "It's almost time to get up!"

He saw that she'd put on a yellow robe. He saw, also, that she had dark smudges under her eyes. "How's the hand? Do you need a pill?"

"It's aching, but I'll skip the painkillers. For now." She crossed to the back door. Opening it, she stood looking out. He could hear the beat of the ocean, but no other sound.

"I love this time of the morning," she murmured. "When everybody's asleep. It's so peaceful."

Glass in hand, he followed her as she stepped outside. To the east, the sky above the rolling hills was faintly streaked with pink. The garden was still. The air hushed.

She padded across the deck and stood with her back to him. As he walked after her, she looked up at the sky and her hair tumbled in a glorious cascade down her back.

Again, he ached to touch.

He gulped down his drink; felt the whiskey fire his blood. But the need for it had gone, burned away by another fire. The fire he felt in his loins, for this woman—this woman he had so slyly manipulated into taking on the job of nanny for his nephew.

When he'd arrived at Number Five to find her sleeping in his house, anger had raged through him. And he'd felt righteous in that anger. She'd sided with Tom and Janine—stubbornly, determinedly, implacably. As far as he was concerned, she'd been the only one who could have stopped the marriage…and instead, she had encouraged it.

She had pitted herself against him. And had won.

And he had wanted revenge.

Now he felt a stab of remorse. A wave of guilt. He'd judged her, without knowing her. He'd thought her hard and aggressive. Dislikable. He'd been wrong. She wasn't the person he'd believed her to be. She was soft, and feminine; compassionate and vulnerable.

But most of all, she was loving.

"Mallory…"

She turned, her face dusky in the dawn shadows. ''Mmm?''

''I'm sorry.''

Something flickered in her eyes. ''Don't be,'' she said quietly. ''All you took was…a friendly kiss.''

He shook his head. ''I'm talking about the way I've treated you—blaming you for Tom and Janine marrying.''

Her expression became wary. ''You've changed your mind about that?''

''I realize now that it was monstrously presumptuous of me to think I could order Janine to have her baby adopted. Keeping the child was her decision to make, not mine. You were right to fight me when I tried to take over. I was wrong about that…and I was wrong about you.''

''But you still resent Tom.'' Her tone was flat.

''From a brother's perspective…yes. He was older, he took advantage of Janine. But it's in the past now. I'm ready to move on. To take responsibility for their baby—''

''Shared responsibility,'' she said quickly. ''We're in this together, remember?''

He grimaced. "On that subject...I have something to tell you."

She stiffened and he knew she'd leaped to the conclusion that he was, in some way, going to shaft her. She still didn't trust him. But could he blame her?

"I have one more apology to make," he said. "When we were discussing custody options, I...tricked you."

She stood completely still. "Go on."

"I warned you then that if you didn't agree to shared custody, I'd take you to court—we both knew I'd win—and then I'd move Matthew to a condo in downtown Seattle and hire a nanny to look after him. It was...a bluff."

"You...*lied?*"

"Yeah."

"But...that was *blackmail.*"

He winced at the incredulity in her tone. And he knew he'd gone down a few notches in her estimation. It surprised him to realize how important it was to him that she *not* think badly of him. Maybe the truth would help...

"It was," he said. "I played dirty. I played on your love for Matthew—I knew that I had you over a barrel and that you'd agree to any terms I proposed, rather than see him moved to the city and cared for by a stranger.''

''But you *detested* me. Why on earth did you go to such ends to keep me in the picture?''

''Because I wanted to be sure Matthew was in good hands, and I could see you were ready-made for the job. Matthew liked you. I figured you'd be the perfect nanny.''

''And now?''

The sun had crept up over the hills and in its rosy light he saw the fine lines fanning from her eyes, the whisper of freckles on her cheeks. Even with anxiety tightening her features, her beauty stole his breath away.

''And now,'' he said softly, ''I like you too, and I figure you'll be the perfect mom.''

At odd moments through the day Mallory found herself thinking about Jordan's double-barreled admission: he liked her and he figured she'd be a perfect mom.

But how would he feel, she wondered, if he ever learned about her deception? Would he still like her? He would certainly no longer think of her as "the perfect mom" for Matthew. In fact, he'd probably toss her out on her ear, which he would have every right to do since Tom was not the baby's father and so she had no blood ties to Janine's baby.

Jordan would never find out, though, because she would never tell him and she was the only person who knew.

That fact should have given her consolation, but it didn't. Nor did it do anything to assuage her feelings of guilt. Guilt that weighed so heavily on her that it must have shown because that evening, as she and Jordan were sitting on the patio after dinner, he said to her,

"You're very quiet. Your hand bothering you?"

She'd taken off her sling after they'd put Matthew to bed, and now she looked down at her bandaged hand. "It was, but I took one of my pills." Then before he could further query her withdrawn mood, she said quickly, "I've been thinking about your nightmares, Jordan, and wondering—do you have them often?"

She'd taken him unawares and she thought she saw him flinch but if he did, he swiftly recovered.

"I have them once in a while." His tone was careless. "But it's no big deal."

"It might help to speak about them."

"Might."

"But you don't want to."

"There's no point." His voice was brusque. "I've had some experiences…not very pleasant experiences…and I dream about them. Talking about it can't change what happened."

"Can't change what happened," she murmured, "but can maybe bring the memories back to the surface—and that can be beneficial. You've stuffed them deeply down inside you where they never see the light of day. But they're there, bursting to get out, and once you're asleep, they escape from their prison and run riot—"

"I said," he shot up from his seat and glared down at her, "I don't want to discuss it."

She dropped her gaze. "I'm sorry." Embarrassment made her cheeks hot. "I thought I might help—"

"Help that's not asked for is interference!"

He spun away from her and marched inside, slamming the door shut with such force the sound reverberated through the house.

Seconds later, Mallory heard a thin wail drifting from Matthew's open bedroom window.

Sighing, she got up and went inside.

Of Jordan, there was no sign.

She crossed the hall and ran lightly upstairs. The baby's cry had begun to tail off by the time she reached the landing, and she slowed her pace as she approached his bedroom door, which she had left ajar.

It now stood wide open.

She halted abruptly when she reached the doorway. Jordan stood at the crib, and he had the baby in his arms. He was rocking him gently, and murmuring to him.

Within a few seconds, the wailing stopped altogether.

She hadn't realized that Jordan was aware of her presence till he was settling Matthew carefully in his crib. Without looking around, he said, in a low voice,

"How many more times do I have to say 'I'm sorry' to you today?" Covering Matthew with a light blanket, he straightened and turned to look at her.

His gray eyes were shadowed with regret.

The sight melted her heart as no words could have.

"I'm sorry too," she said as he crossed to her. "I was thoughtless. Tactless."

They walked along the passage to the stairs.

"You were being kind." He stopped with his hand on the railing. "And I responded by being rude."

"You were entitled."

As he made to move on, she said, "Just one more thing."

"Yeah?"

"I won't bring up the subject again, now that I know how you feel about it. But if you should ever want to talk about it, Jordan, I'll be here to listen."

As he lay in bed that night, Mallory's words came back to him.

And he remembered the way her brown eyes had softened with compassion as she'd looked up at him.

He'd wanted to draw her into his arms, hold her close. Not for any sexual purposes, but just for the comfort he knew he would draw from such an embrace.

But that would have been selfish. She'd admitted she found him attractive, and he knew she was drawn to him, sexually. But it would be wrong to encourage her, wrong to start something that he was not prepared to finish. A woman like her deserved a man who believed in love and commitment.

He was a man who believed in neither.

Next morning, over breakfast, he said to her, "We'd better look into getting a lawyer today."

She lowered her coffee mug. "I forgot to tell you—James is a lawyer. When he and Dee were here the other day, I happened to mention our plans, and he offered to draw up our agreement while he's here. For free."

"I'm not into freebies!" He scowled at her, tried not to be distracted by how pretty she looked. She was wearing a green-and-white striped halter top with perky green shorts, while her loose hair shone like polished copper. "And I prefer not to mix business with friendship...James *is* your friend, isn't he?" Without waiting for a response, he went on,

"I'll check the Yellow Pages, find a lawyer there."

She chuckled. "You won't need the Yellow Pages. There's only one lawyer in Seashore— Jacob Pritchard—and he's at home recovering from prostate surgery."

"Where's the nearest town?"

"Larch Grove."

"We'll drive over there and—"

"Oh, don't be so *difficult,* Jordan! It's not going to *kill* you to let James do the work. And if you insist on paying—" she watched as he started to pace the kitchen "—well, I'm not about to stop you."

He paced the room three times before turning to her with the thwarted expression of a child who's just been told he *has* to have his booster shots. "What's Elsa's number?"

Within moments he was talking to James— at least, it seemed that James was the one doing most of the talking.

After he hung up, Jordan stuck his hands on his hips and looked at her grimly.

"This is not the way I like to do business, Mallory!"

She raised her eyebrows. "Problems?"

"James insists we have our meeting at Elsa's," he said through gritted teeth. "He's set it up for this evening. We're to go there at five for a barbecue—Elsa's having some other friends over—and after, Elsa will baby-sit while we talk with James."

"Sounds like fun!"

"Sounds like a recipe for a headache."

"You really should lighten up." She refilled his coffee mug. "Barbecues at Elsa's can be a blast. But perish the thought," she added mockingly, "that you might actually enjoy yourself!"

Mallory snuck a sideways glance at Jordan as they walked along the sidewalk to Elsa's at five o'clock. He was looking devastatingly attractive in a navy-and-white checked shirt and chinos—but he was not a happy camper.

He was wheeling Matthew's stroller, but his attention was not on the baby, who was waving a rattle at him. His brow was furrowed, his eyes glazed, his lips compressed.

"If I'd realized that doing business with James was going to make you so infernally grumpy,'' she said, ''I'd have let you go to Larch Grove!''

''Turning James down,'' he said, ''wasn't an option.''

''I didn't see anyone twisting your arm!''

''No—'' his lips twisted in an ironic smile ''—you didn't, did you!''

The man was behaving *very* oddly. He'd made it abundantly clear he didn't want to go to the barbecue yet he'd gone to pains to spruce himself up. After their talk, he'd walked along to town and come back with a great haircut. Then around four o'clock, after spending an hour in the attic fixing the broken window, he'd gone out to his car and brought in an enormous battered leather suitcase.

When she saw it, she said, ''What's that?''

''A suitcase,'' he deadpanned.

''I know what it is! What I meant was…well, it's so big!''

''You've heard of people who live out of a suitcase? I'm one of 'em. This contains all my worldly goods.''

''*All* your worldly goods?''

''Yup. Except for the car, which I keep garaged at a lockup in Seattle.''

Mallory's mind boggled as she mentally stacked his one case alongside all the boxes and furniture she'd had moved here from Seattle. And she'd thought *she* lived frugally!

"Why are you bringing it in now?" she asked.

"I need slacks and a shirt to wear to the barbecue."

"Go as you are. You're fine. It'll be very casual."

He looked down at his dusty tank top and swiped at the spiderwebs on his jeans. "There's a difference between casual and grunge." He ran his gaze assessingly over her. "You're not going like that, are you?"

"Well, yes, I—"

"You need to have a shower—wash your hair, get changed."

She put her hand defensively to her head. "My hair's okay—"

"Your hair," he said, "is straggly. You've been out in the garden most of the day and you got all sweated up—"

"I can't shower."

"Put your hand in a plastic bag. And after, if you need help getting dressed, I'll help."

Oh, sure…as if she'd let him within ten feet of her if she was naked! "Thank you," she said, "but I'll manage."

And she *had* managed, though everything took six times as long as usual. The one thing she couldn't do was fasten her bra. So in the end, rather than ask Jordan's help, she'd decided to go braless. And because of that, she'd chosen to wear her crisp blue shirt with her white pedal-pushers, rather than the clinging knit top she'd have preferred—

"Is this Elsa's place?" Jordan asked.

Mallory glanced at the rambling two-storey house. "Mmm, this is it."

They walked up the drive together, but as she made for the front door, he said,

"We'll go in the back."

Mallory rolled her eyes. Bossy, bossy!

He opened the side gate and stood aside to let her enter.

She stepped into the garden…and stopped short. A dozen people stood on the patio. Pink, blue and yellow balloons decorated the trees. And a garish red sign was suspended from the clothes line. It read:

WELCOME TO SEASHORE, MALLORY.

Stunned, she just stood there, till Jordan pushed her forward.

As he did, they all laughed, and shouted: Surprise!

CHAPTER NINE

THE PARTY had apparently been in the works for weeks.

"We just wanted you to know," Meg said, as she scooped Matthew from his stroller, "how *happy* we all are that you've finally moved here permanently."

"It cost us, though!" James had a mischievous gleam in his eyes. "Elsa had us all club together and buy you a housewarming gift."

"Garden-warming, actually." Sam smiled. "It's for the backyard—a blue and yellow swing and teeter-totter set. Steel. Top-of-the-line. It'll be great for Matthew."

"And for the day care too," Elsa put in. "In my humble opinion, children like nothing better than to play on a swing!"

"Sears will be delivering the set tomorrow." Dee ushered Mallory over to a lawn chair while the sisters clustered around Meg and the baby. "Give us a call after it arrives and James will pop over and help Jordan set it up.''

Mallory felt overwhelmed by the kindness showered on her. But even as she thanked everyone, she spared a thought for Jordan, who had moved to the fringe of the crowd. Though he looked cheerful enough, she knew it had to be an act. This kind of ''down-home do'' was anathema to him. She'd have to tell him, at the first opportunity, that she really appreciated his letting himself be roped in.

The opportunity didn't arise till some time later. Because it was a lovely evening, they had all sat around chatting after the barbecue— Elsa, James, Dee, Meg, Jordan and the sisters at one picnic table, Mallory at the other with Tyler Scott, Dave Matlock of Matlock's Marina, and several others she'd come to know over the past months.

It was only when she noticed Jordan get up and amble into the house around eight o'clock that she saw her chance. She waited a couple of minutes and then followed him inside.

She found him in the sitting room. He was crouched at a low bookcase crammed with mystery novels; travel books; and the hardback biographies of World War II heroes—dusty tomes collected by Elsa's late husband.

"Jordan?"

He got up and turned. "You're ready to leave?"

"No. I just wanted to say—about coming here—someone *did* twist your arm, didn't they! When you called James this morning, he told you about the party and delegated you to get me here on time. I'm sorry you were put in that position."

"No problem. It was in a good cause."

"I admit I was puzzled after that phone call—it appeared that you'd let James steamroller you into doing business *his* way and on his terms...and you hadn't struck me as the type to let *anyone* tell you what to do."

His gray eyes took on a cynical glint. "Nobody's ever accused me of being a doormat."

She laughed. "You did a good job of fooling me—then, and on the way over here too. I had no idea you were involved in a major cover-up! I have to thank you," she went on, "for making me shower and change. At least I look presentable. All those photos Meg took—"

"You look more than presentable."

The words, though quietly spoken, had an intensity that charged the atmosphere and exploded their casual rapport. His eyes had darkened...and their expression said: *You look fantastic.* Her heartbeats slid into a dangerous skid and her throat tightened. But she managed to parry with a light: "You look more than presentable yourself!"

And wasn't that the truth! She'd been painfully aware of him all evening—

He came towards her with sexual intent preceding him in almost palpable waves. Heartbeats hammering, she fought a rise of panic. "Another thing," she tried to step back but to her dismay, came up against the doorjamb, "I have to congratulate you on your behaviour."

He raised a mocking eyebrow. "You mean because—unlike Matthew—I didn't spill my drink on Angelina's dress or make a damp stain on Elsa's lap or—"

She had to chuckle. "No, of course not. Jordan, you could have been a party-pooper, but instead, you pretended to be having a good time. I know you hate this kind of get-together.

Janine used to talk about you—about your likes and dislikes—''

''She did?'' His eyes were hooded as he gazed down at her. ''So…which of my other secrets did she give away?''

Mallory caught the faintest hint of his after-shave. Not a punchy in-your-face scent, but something complex and subtly sensual. It made her think dreamily of dancing with him, of pressing her lips to his smooth cheek—

''What's wrong?'' With a questioning look, he rubbed the heel of his hand over that smooth cheek. ''Do I have barbecue sauce dribbling down my—''

''No.'' But the temptation to touch was too powerful to resist. She reached up her right hand and ran the tip of her index finger over the angular slash of his cheekbone. ''It's only a crumb from Elsa's lemon pie,'' she fibbed, reveling in the intimacy of the moment, before brushing away the imaginary crumb.

''There,'' she said—and drew in a tiny gasp as he caught her wrist.

''Tell me,'' he said softly, ''what else Janine said about me.''

His smouldering gray gaze was hypnotic. She couldn't have drawn herself away if she'd wanted to. Which she didn't. "Janine said you hated small towns, because you were brought up in a small town—"

"Nowhere, U.S.A." His laugh was sardonic.

"And you detested everybody knowing everybody else's business—"

"What I detested," he said, drawing her hand to his lips and trailing a kiss over her inner wrist, "was everybody knowing my *family's* business."

Did he feel the quiver that ran from her wrist to her toes? He must have! To her, it had felt like the tremor of an earthquake. "And why did you hate that so much?" she asked huskily.

"Because my father cheated on my mother. And let's not forget their ugly divorce or the fact that my mother died before it went through and my father remarried within days of her death— married the woman he'd been having an adulterous affair with for years, a woman I hated. And they were the talk of the town…"

He kissed her neck and she stiffened. He kissed it again, and she arched her head back with a moan. "The woman he married was a brassy redhead. And what even Janine didn't know was that I had to lock my bedroom door to keep her out. Ever since then," he slid his hands to her nape, "I've hated redheads. Till now. You," he murmured, "have the most beautiful hair I've ever seen." Spreading his fingers, he swept them voluptuously through the silky mass. "I could wrap myself up in it, lose myself..."

Mallory heard an odd whimpering sound...and realized, with a shock, that it had come from her own throat.

"This," he whispered, bringing his mouth close to hers, "is not a good idea. I've told myself to keep away from you, not to get involved. But here we are—"

He kissed her full on the mouth and stole any protest she might have made. Not that she was capable of making any! She was totally lost in sensation. Lost in the taste of his breath, the warmth of his lips, the pressure of his body against hers...and the urgency of his desire...

Matched by her own. She felt herself spinning out of control as she returned his kiss with a wanton eagerness—

"Mallory?" Meg's voice sounded very near and Mallory automatically jerked her mouth from Jordan's. But even as she tried to pull away from him, he slid an arm tightly around her waist and kept her in place. Before she could struggle from his grasp, Meg appeared in the doorway.

"Oh, there you are!" Meg seemed amused rather than surprised to find them together. "I just came to tell you that Matthew's awake...and he's growly."

Jordan spoke before Mallory could suck enough breath into her lungs to respond. "Thanks, Meg," he said. "We'll be there in a sec."

Meg took off and Mallory made to follow her, but Jordan tightened his grip and swung her around to face him.

"Why are you embarrassed? We weren't doing anything wrong, Mallory. Did it feel wrong to you?"

Nothing had ever felt more right. "I don't like having Meg think we snuck in here to indulge in a kissing spree—nothing could be further from the truth! The only reason I followed you in here was so I could thank you.''

''You haven't answered my question.'' He fixed her with a steady gaze. ''*Did* it feel wrong to you?''

From outside drifted a loud wail from Matthew.

''Excuse me,'' she said quickly, grasping the excuse to avoid answering him. ''I have to go and tend to the baby.''

Cheeks burning, she slid free from his grip and hurried back outside.

The party broke up soon after, as Matthew wouldn't settle.

While guests drifted out of the yard, Jordan watched Dee nestle the cranky child in the stroller.

''I think he may be teething again,'' Elsa suggested over the baby's restless grumbling. ''He's been rubbing his gum.''

''You're probably right.'' Mallory touched Matthew's cheek. ''Look at this red patch...it wasn't there earlier.''

James walked to the end of the drive with them.

"We didn't get that contract done," he said, "but we'll work on it tomorrow when I come over to help with the swing set. Do you still have Tom's tools, Mallory?"

"Yes, they're in the workshop."

"Good." James lifted his hand in a salute. "See you tomorrow, then."

As Jordan wheeled the stroller along the street towards Number Five, with Mallory stepping briskly beside him, he felt tension crackling between them—and it had been crackling ever since the kiss.

Not that she hadn't enjoyed it—if her response had been anything to go by, she'd enjoyed it as much as he had. And though on that other occasion he'd limited himself to a fleeting kiss because he hadn't wanted to take advantage of her, he was beginning to rethink that philosophy. He still didn't want to hurt her, but since neither of them was interested in marriage, surely there would be no harm in a no-strings affair, especially if they both entered into it with their eyes open? They could keep their relationship discreet...and it would be great for him to have a warm bed waiting when he visited in the future.

He believed the lady would be willing…but she was nervous. He would have to move slowly. Like a sensitive filly, she needed careful handling. He had to work at gaining her confidence. And a good time to start would be now.

"It's a beautiful evening," he said pleasantly. And it was. The setting sun painted a glowing bronze path over the water, and several yachts with vividly-coloured sails skimmed like butterflies over the surface on their way home.

"Yes," Mallory said. "But it's cooled off quite a bit."

Just as she had! "I heard Tyler ask you to go sailing on Friday." He kept his tone casual. "Did you accept?"

"Not this time."

"Too bad. I'd have baby-sat—"

"That wouldn't have been necessary."

"I'd have enjoyed it."

The wind caught her hair and she put up hand to keep it off her face. "You've changed," she said dryly. "When you got here, you couldn't even be bothered looking at him.''

''I thought babies were…well, just babies! I'd never realized they were little persons, with their own distinct personalities.'' He looked down at Matthew, who was trying to stick his fists into his mouth. ''We're buddies. The bond is truly amazing…but I guess it's because we're kin.''

He glanced back at Mallory and caught a strange look in her eyes. It was gone in a flash, and she said lightly, ''Blood ties, they're all-important to you, aren't they!''

''That's what family's all about,'' he said. And as Matthew broke into a wail, he added with an ironic grin, ''That's why you and I are going to spend the next twenty years sharing custody of this delightful little tyke!''

Delightful wasn't the word Mallory would have applied to Matthew when he woke her at midnight with his fretty crying.

She'd been in a deep sleep, and by the time she roused herself, dragged on her robe, and stumbled through to the baby's room, she found Jordan was already there. He was wearing only a pair of dark checked boxer shorts, and he was holding Matthew up, checking his diaper.

"Dry," he said, when he saw her. "So that's not the problem."

He nestled the baby against his shoulder and tried to rub his back but Matthew wailed even more shrilly.

Mallory saw that his left cheek was scarlet, his eyes sparkling with tears.

"I'll go downstairs," she said over his cries, "and warm him a bottle. Be back in a few minutes."

As she hurried down the stairs, she felt dizzy—not in a reaction to seeing Jordan half-naked, but a reaction to seeing him with the baby. On the surface, he appeared rock-hard and tough; but inside, he was tender and compassionate.

And that had touched her soul. She'd never felt like this about a man before—this moon-struck lovesick way....

*Love*sick?

The thought almost stopped her heart! She halted abruptly at the foot of the stairs and grabbed the top of the newel post to steady herself. Was it possible that she had, after all, fallen in love with Jordan Caine?

Was *that* why she couldn't keep her eyes off him? Was *that* why she melted when he touched her? Was that why she couldn't stop thinking about him?

But I don't *want* to be in love with him! she thought frantically. I don't want to give my heart to a man like him—a man who flits around the world and puts down no roots. A man who calls no place home.

She stood there for a long giddy moment, as she struggled against the possibility...before, in the end, accepting that it wasn't just a possibility, it was fact. She'd fallen in love with the man. Wildly, crazily, permanently. And she could do absolutely nothing about it.

Feeling as dazed as if she'd been on a runaway roller-coaster, she dropped her hand from the post and made her way to the kitchen, her thoughts in a turmoil.

As she warmed the baby's milk, she used the time to gather herself together. It took several minutes. And when she went back upstairs, she'd steeled herself to resist his attraction—and had convinced herself she could pull it off.

But the moment she saw him sprawled in the rocking chair by the crib sound asleep, with the baby dozing in his arms, her traitorous heart turned to mush.

He had never looked more vulnerable; more endearing. She ached to tiptoe over, to brush a kiss over his lips, weave her fingers through that disheveled hair—

Instead, she set the baby's bottle on the dresser. And dragging her gaze from this man who had unknowingly stolen her heart, she left the room and returned to her own.

Sears delivered the swing set the following afternoon.

It took Jordan and James an hour to put the parts together and erect it. The day was very hot and sticky and by the time they'd finished, Jordan was more than ready for the iced tea Mallory brought out to the patio.

"When Matthew wakes from his nap," she said as they sat around the patio table, "we'll tuck him into one of the little swings." She passed around a plate of sugar cookies. "He's going to love it!"

"How's he been today?" James asked.

"Another tooth broke through," Jordan said. "He's feeling better now but he had us up through the night."

"So I slept in this morning," Mallory said. "And when I came down, Jordan had already fed him and changed him."

"Getting to be quite the dad!" James said with a laugh.

"Hey, Mallory actually allowed me to bathe him today," Jordan shot back. "Although I could see that the experience was more traumatic for her than for me!"

"Well, Matthew's so slippy!" Mallory protested. "And let's face it," she added with a laugh, "he did almost get away on you once."

James gulped down a few thirsty mouthfuls of his iced tea, and then sat back in his chair. "Okay," he said. "Let's get down to business."

Jordan and Mallory filled him in on what they had decided to do about the baby and his future and James assured them that since Mallory had already cut through all the preliminary red tape during the past few months, there should be no hiccups ahead.

"But both of you," he said finally, "should plan to update your wills soon. Mallory wouldn't have had to go through all these bureaucratic hoops if Tom and Janine had written a will, declaring you guardians of their expected child in the event that anything should happen to them…"

Mallory rose clumsily from her seat. "Excuse me, I'm going up to check on Matthew."

Jordan frowned as she went inside. Her voice had had a faint tremor, and he thought he'd seen the gleam of tears in her eyes.

He waited till she was out of earshot before he said quietly to James, "Mallory's been under a lot of pressure lately. I want her to feel secure, and it's just occurred to me how I can make that happen." He leaned forward in his seat and planted his elbows on the table. "Here's what I need you to do…."

After James had left, Jordan went inside. Mallory wasn't around so he went upstairs to look for her. She wasn't in the baby's room— and Matthew was still asleep.

Her bedroom door was ajar and as he passed it, he heard a muffled sound inside.

He rapped lightly on the door. "Mallory?"

The sound stopped.

"May I come in?" Without thinking, he pushed the door open and saw her at the window. She didn't turn as he entered the room. Her shoulders were hunched, and when he heard the muffled sound again, he realized she was crying.

Feeling helpless, he walked over to her. "Mallory?" He brought her to face him. "What's wrong?"

She took a few moments to gather some composure. "It's Tom." Her voice was ragged, and she dabbed her eyes with a tissue. "And Janine. Sometimes I think I'm...you know, getting over things...at least a bit...and then, all of a sudden, I just feel swamped...with grief."

"It was talking with James," he said, "that did it." He felt a pang of compassion when he saw that her eyes were red-rimmed, her cheeks blotchy. "There we were, talking about their baby—dividing up our responsibilities—"

"Yes," she gulped, "that was just it. It made me feel so sad that Tom and Janine aren't here to enjoy Matthew. They both went through a lot and they deserved to be happy." She dabbed her eyes again.

"It'll take time."

"That's what everybody says. But I wonder if the pain will ever go away."

"Maybe it'll never go away," he said softly. "But over time, it will ease."

She took in a deep breath, and he saw that she was calmer. "Yes," she said. "You're probably right."

He cocked his head as he heard the baby cry out. "Matthew's awake," he said. "Let's show him his new swing set. And this evening, I'm taking you out to dinner."

"No, I can't—"

"It was James's idea. He said he and Dee would come along and baby-sit. It'll do you good," he added, over her protests. "Cheer you up. We'll drive out to the Golf and Country Club—apparently that's where James and Dee had their wedding reception, and he recommends it highly."

"No, I can't, Jordan. I have to go along to the clinic later. Tyler wants to have a look at my hand."

"What time's your appointment?"

"Five-thirty."

"No problem...I'll book a table for seven o'clock. In the meantime," he said, "let's take our nephew outside and show him what a lucky little boy he is!"

Tyler Scott ran a fingertip lightly over Mallory's scar. "Looking good," he murmured. "It's healing nicely." He tossed her bandage into his garbage can and put on another. "So," he said as he washed his hands, "what's on your agenda tonight?"

"Jordan and I are going out to the Country Club for dinner."

"I didn't expect to like the guy, after the way he left you to cope alone with the baby, all these months. But," he dried his hands briskly, "he seemed...solid. Did you find out why he didn't come back sooner?"

Mallory got up from her seat. "No. It's a mystery. But I agree...he does *seem* solid."

"He fancies you." Tyler flicked back a lock of his blond hair. And grinned. "Not that I blame him. But maybe he'll have more luck than I. I noticed last night that you were having a hard job keeping your eyes off him."

Had she been so transparent? "He's good-looking." She lifted her shoulders in a careless shrug. "I won't deny it."

"I've been told I'm not half-bad-looking myself," he said impudently, "but you've never stared at me like that!"

She chuckled. "Dr. Scott, let me remind you that you can land in serious trouble if you flirt with a patient."

"Ms. Madison," he said with a wicked smile, "let me remind you that you can land in even more serious trouble if you let yourself fall in love with a man like Jordan Caine!"

Cool and reserved: that was the impression Mallory wanted to give on their dinner date. And she bore that in mind when she chose to wear a simple turquoise dress. And because her hair was obviously such a temptation to him, she scraped it back—as best she could, given that her left hand wasn't very agile—and twisted it into a severe chignon. For makeup, she allowed only a hint of peach lipstick, the lightest brushing of dusky eyeshadow, and lastly she applied the most delicate spritzing of perfume to her pulse points.

The doorbell chimed as she was slipping on her stiletto shoes. After giving herself a quick check in the mirror, she peeked into Matthew's room to make sure he was asleep, and then walked along the passage to the landing.

When she reached it, she saw that Jordan had already brought Dee and James in.

Oh, boy.

She held on to the railing as she stared down at him. He was wearing a gray suit, an ice-blue shirt, and a tie with a gray-and-blue pattern. He looked devastating!

Drawing herself together, she started down the stairs. ''Hi, there!'' she called. ''You're right on time!''

After Dee and James greeted her, she glanced at Jordan again and felt her pulse stagger. He was gazing at her with a dazed expression. As if someone had come up behind him and pressed a gun to his back. Well, that makes two of us, she could have told him. I feel just as bedazzled when I look at you!

"The air's very still," Dee said. "Do you think there's a storm brewing?"

An electrical one for sure, Mallory thought wryly. And she was going to have to be careful or she'd get fried.

"It may pass over," James was saying. "In any case, you don't have far to go."

"Matthew's in the upstairs bedroom, Dee," Mallory said. "I doubt he'll waken before we get back, but if he does, give him some juice. His bottle's in the fridge."

"Don't worry," Dee said. "Just go out and enjoy yourselves. You'll have a wonderful meal at the Club."

Mallory drank the last few drops of the perfect coffee and sat back in her seat. "Dee was right," she murmured, as she put down her serviette. "That was a superb meal, Jordan. Thank you."

"My pleasure." The lavishly-furnished dining room looked out over the eighteenth green, and as Jordan glanced out, he saw lightning flash over the fast-darkening sky. At the same time, heavy raindrops spattered the window-panes.

"Storm's going to hit," he said. "Let's go." He paid their bill and then ushered Mallory outside, through the foyer with its glassed-in shelves of trophies. Over a peal of thunder, he called, "We'll have to make a run for it."

No sooner had they got into the car than the rain started in earnest.

"What a downpour," Mallory said in awe as she sank back in her seat. "And getting worse by the second..."

"Yup." He set the Lexus in motion, "Not a night to be out, for sure!" The rain pounded on the roof with such force they could have been under Niagara Falls.

They drove without talking for about five minutes, the road awash and hissing in the lashing deluge. But when the windshield wipers lost their battle to keep up with the torrential onslaught, Jordan said, "I can hardly see a damned thing—I'm going to pull in till the storm passes."

"There's a picnic area around here somewhere." Mallory peered out her side window. "Oh—there it is."

He swerved off the road and splashed the car into the little picnic area. Braking to a halt, he parked, switched off the lights, and leaned sideways against his door.

''Well.'' Mallory took in a deep breath; let out a long shaky one. ''Here we are. Safe and sound.''

Sound she might be, Jordan thought; safe she most definitely was not! Not with him...

In the shadowy dark, he could see only her outline. But her image was burnt into his mind—the prim chignon, the discreetly-glossed lips, the demurely-attired figure. The unspoken message: This lady's not for touching....

It was a message, he mused wryly, that both his brain and his body stubbornly ignored. The more the delectable Ms. Madison tried to play down her assets, the more he desired her. All evening, he'd yearned to unravel that glorious hair, claim those pouty lips, caress that luscious figure.

And get close enough to lose himself in that tantalizing perfume, which along with her musky pheromones, had been driving him crazy ever since they left the house.

As if she'd been reading his mind, she shifted nervously in her seat. Away from him.

"So," she said warily, "what do we do now?"

He chuckled. "What a couple usually does," he drawled, "when they're trapped together, in a storm, in the dark."

CHAPTER TEN

TENSION skittered between them.

"Talk?" Mallory's tone was arch.

He laughed, and his laughter eased the moment.

"Sure." Lazily, he rested his elbow on the back of his seat. "What else could I mean?"

"What do you want to talk about?"

"Your choice." His eyes had adjusted to the dark and he saw she was looking at him.

"Let's talk about you."

"My favourite subject," he said with dry humour. "But I thought Janine had filled you in—"

"She didn't speak much about your work. I know you have a mining-exploration company—"

"Goldriver Drilling Inc."

"How did you get your start? Janine said you finished high school but you didn't go on to college."

"After I graduated, I meant to take just a year off, but in the end...well, I never went back. I headed up to Alaska, landed a job with an old geezer who had his own drilling company. He took a shine to me—we were two of a kind, both loners—and he taught me the ropes."

"You enjoyed the work?"

"Oh, yeah. And in my spare time, I panned for gold. Was lucky enough to hit it rich—at least, rich enough that when Fred retired a few years later, I was able to buy the company. And after that, because I'd developed itchy feet, and also enjoyed an element of risk, I started contracting to drill at mining sites abroad, in developing nations—"

"And that's how you ended up in Zlobovia?"

"Yeah." He didn't want to talk about Zlobovia, or his contract with Brokaw Mining to drill at one of their sites deep in rebel country. Nor did he want to talk about Niall Brokaw, the company president, whose distraught wife had come to him, begging for help, the very day he was preparing to fly home for Janine's funeral.

Deliberately driving the conversation off at a slant, he said, ''The job's financially rewarding, enough so that I don't have any money worries.''

''That must be nice.'' She said it in a matter-of-fact way, with no trace of envy or even wistfulness in her tone.

''What's nice is the independence that comes with it. Because I'm my own boss, I'm at liberty to pick up and go, whenever I please. And you can't put a price on that.''

''How different we are,'' she mused. ''I need roots. You want freedom.''

He'd never wanted it as much, nor valued it as much, as during those eight months when he didn't have it. And from the moment he'd escaped from his captors, he'd appreciated liberty with an intensity that was soul-deep.

But if he hated being tied down...then why wasn't he feeling restless in his current situation—''trapped'' into staying on at Number Five when he'd intended staying only one night? Why wasn't he chafing under the restraints—because there were indeed restraints! Perhaps not visible ones such as those that had confined him in that sunbaked hellhole, but in-

visible ones. Ties that were as fine as gossa-
mer, yet sticky as a spider web.

Family ties.

Now there was a thought to strike terror into
a man whose main aim in life was to remain
free as a sparrow—

Lightning flashed, and seconds later, thunder cracked, the reverberating boom all but
shaking the car. He glanced at Mallory and
saw her cringe. Rain still pounded the roof
mercilessly and he had to raise his voice over
the drumming sound as he said, ''Are you
Okay?''

She answered but he couldn't hear. Moving
over, he slid his arm across the back of her
seat.

''Sorry.'' He bent his head. ''I didn't
catch—''

''I'm not afraid in storms—but I have to admit, this one is a bit overwhelming.''

As was her perfume. The heat of her body,
or perhaps her nervousness, had added an exotic wildness to the amber Oriental fragrance,
and it occurred to him that if he'd been standing, the potent sensuality of it might have
brought him to his knees.

"Don't worry," he murmured. "You're safe here."

He itched to tug the tortoiseshell pins from her chignon. Instead, he restrained himself and said, "So, what else do you want to know about me?"

She paused for a beat before saying, "You've never been married. And you say marriage isn't in your future either. But of course you've had relationships."

"Oh, yeah." His tone was ironic. "I've had my share."

"You must have left a trail of broken hearts behind."

"A backhanded compliment." He chuckled. "But if I did," he went on with a shrug in his voice, "the ladies had only themselves to blame. I've always made it clear to my paramours that my intentions aren't honourable."

"That woman—the one you took off with in Zlobovia—did *she* know what kind of a man she was dealing with?"

"Sarcasm doesn't suit you, Mallory." Why the *hell* was she so determined to pry into that episode? "But yes," he continued curtly.

"She did. She knew it perfectly well. And that was why she…wanted my services."

Thunder rolled overhead. She waited till it had passed, before saying, "Where is she now?"

In the flash of lightning that followed the thunder, he saw a challenging glint in her eyes. It provoked him into snapping back, "She's with her husband, sweetheart, and their two children."

Her eyes widened in shock. "You were having an affair with a married—"

"No, I was damned well not having an affair with a married woman! Good God, I've told you about my father, do you think I'd ever be part of such a betrayal, after watching how his affairs destroyed our family? One thing you should know about me—I *despise* anyone…man or woman…who gets involved in an adulterous relationship. No," he amended harshly, "despise isn't a strong enough word. I have nothing but the utmost *contempt*—"

She made an odd little gulping sound—like a sob—and he broke off with a curse. Dammit, he'd upset her…again. But why had he let her get to him like that? Why had he turned his bitterness against her, when she was innocent of any wrong? Turning roughly away from her, he grabbed the steering wheel. And after a long tense moment, he said, with a heavy sigh, "I'm sorry."

But it was too late. In a flat tone that shut out any further conversation, she said,

"The rain's not as heavy now. It should be safe to get back on the road."

He didn't want to get back on the road. He wanted to shove open the car door and stride blindly out into the storm. Wanted to walk, and walk, as if the rain could wash away the past. But he knew it could never do that.

He switched on the engine and got back onto the road.

And they didn't speak one more word to each other, all the way home.

She could *never* tell him about Janine.

Not that she'd been planning to. But if it had ever crossed her mind, Mallory reflected as she climbed into bed that night, she now knew it was *totally* out of the question. Jordan had declared that he had nothing but the ut-most contempt for anyone who became involved in an adulterous affair. And Janine had been guilty of doing just that. She'd been young, and she'd been immature…and she had been a victim. The man—a college lecturer— had seduced her and had stolen her innocence. But Jordan would never see it that way. Bitterness blinded him. He would believe she was just like their father and find her behaviour unforgivable.

Janine had known that. And that was why she had so desperately wanted him never to find out the truth.

Which had left Mallory as sole guardian of Janine's secret—sworn to silence, so that Jordan's memories of his sister would remain forever unsullied.

That night, she heard him cry out in his sleep. And she knew he was having his nightmare again. This time, she didn't get up and hurry to him. She turned over onto her stomach, buried her face in her pillow, and stayed that way till the house returned, once more, to quiet.

During the next several days, she and Jordan fell into a routine—looking after the baby together, playing with him, taking him for walks, pottering about the house and garden while he dozed during his naps.

But although Jordan seemed to find their relationship easy and comfortable, Mallory felt constantly on edge. And she found herself not only fantasizing about him during the day, but dreaming restlessly about him when she slept.

Five nights after his previous nightmare, she heard him cry out again. Once again, she turned over in her bed, buried her face in her pillow, and tried to sleep. But her efforts were in vain. She tossed and turned, but when she did doze off, it was fitfully, and she woke again, early.

She got up, showered and dressed, and when she went out to the passage, saw that Jordan's door was still closed.

She took Matthew downstairs, fed him, and had just put on the coffee when Jordan ambled into the kitchen.

He was wearing khaki shorts and a khaki shirt, and the rugged outfit accentuated his masculinity. She found herself comparing him to Tyler, whose idea of "casual" was a pair of Armani pants and a silk Ralph Lauren cardigan!

"Hi," he said. And skimming a glance over her, added casually, "You look *great* in that colour."

Flushing, Mallory glanced at the periwinkle T-shirt tucked into her jeans. "Thanks." She didn't tell him that the reason she'd worn the shirt was that she *knew* she looked great in it. Pure vanity. Foolish vanity! The man hadn't spared her a sideways glance since their dinner outing...yet perversely, she'd wanted to look her best.

He'd already turned his attention to Matthew. Leaning over the high chair, he ruffled the baby's blond hair affectionately, and then child and uncle exchanged several moments of baby talk, before he turned back to her again.

He'd had a rough night, Mallory mused, as she noticed the strained look in his eyes. And she felt a pang of guilt that she hadn't gone to him, comforted him when he'd cried out. But she'd been afraid to. Afraid not of him, but of herself. Of her vulnerability to him.

"Sit down," she said. "I'll pour your coffee. Would you like bacon and eggs?"

"That'd be terrific." He took a seat and glanced up at her as she set a mug of coffee before him. "So...what are your plans for the day?"

"I have a couple of moms coming over this morning to talk about the day care."

"I'll take Matthew off your hands."

"You don't have to—the moms will be bringing their toddlers with them."

"I don't want to be around for that. I'll take off before they come, take a walk along to town. Matt'll be company for me."

Matt. That was the first time anyone had referred to the baby by the shortened version of his name. She liked it.

"How's the hand today?" he asked.

"Oh, it's fine now. I can take the bandage off tomorrow—I'll be able to get a rubber glove on then, and be able to bathe the baby. But could you bathe him this morning as usual, after you've had your breakfast?"

"Be glad to," he said as she took eggs and bacon from the fridge. "So...I guess you won't be needing me around, after tomorrow."

She didn't want to think about that. Didn't want to think about how she was going to miss him. "No, you'll be free to leave." She set the frying pan on the stove. "Any idea where you'll be going?"

"Australia."

Australia! He might as well be going to another planet. Mallory hid her dismay as she said, "You have something in the works already?"

"Nothing definite, but I've made a few calls and I have a meeting lined up next week with a guy in Sydney. Looks like a go."

"You'll be there a while?"

"A few months. Or even years. It could turn out to be long-term. This guy has vast interests Down Under."

"So you might end up settling there?" Turning her back on him in case her distress showed in her expression, she concentrated on laying strips of bacon in the pan.

"I've told you, sweetheart—" his tone was flippant "—home is where I hang my hat. And I don't own a hat!"

Swallowing back the lump in her throat, she said, in an equally flippant tone, "You could always get one. I think I could see you in an Akubra.'' She had a swift mental image of Jordan wearing the quintessential Aussie hat made of rabbit fur felt. ''You'd cut a dashing figure!''

Matt leaned over his chair and deliberately dropped his rattle to the floor. Then he turned his head and fixed his uncle with an unblinking ''Your move!'' expression.

Jordan laughed. Scooping up the rattle, he set it on the plastic tray.

Without taking his eyes from Jordan, the baby picked it up and dropped it again.

Jordan laughed again. ''It's a game, right?'' he said to Mallory as he handed Matt the rattle.

''Oh yes.'' She moved the sizzling bacon around with her spatula. ''And it can go on for hours.'' She glanced around. ''If you like, you can pop him outside in his playpen—I've set it up on the patio.''

''Okay, will do.''

When he came back inside, Mallory said, ''Will this be your first time in Australia?''

''No, I've been there twice. It's a fabulous country—you'd love it.''

She just smiled.

"I can see them already." He leaned against the counter and watched as she flipped his eggs over.

She turned with a faint frown tucking her eyebrows together. "See what?"

He nodded towards her feet. "Your roots. They're starting to dig in."

Confusion clouded her eyes for a moment, and then she laughed. "That obvious, huh?"

"Well, you did say roots were what you wanted. Needed. Any particular reason?"

"Oh, it's because when I was growing up we never had a place of our own. A place to call home. Things were different for you—you lived in the same house till you finished high school—and your folk owned it—so I suppose you took that security for granted. But my father was shiftless—we seemed to be constantly on the move—and more often than not they were moonlight flittings. I hated it. I used to dream of having a real home—nothing grand, just four walls and a roof, but the deed would have my name on it." She took a heated plate from the oven. Spreading the bacon strips on it, she added, "That's something I wouldn't expect you to understand."

"You're wrong, Mallory. I do understand how you feel."

"It was just a dream, of course," she said absently as she set his plate on the table. "Even when I was working in Seattle and taking in a decent enough salary, I knew it would never happen. The price of houses nowadays..." She shook her head, and slid a plate of hot buttered toast onto the table. "But still, it's always fun to dream."

Her dream was going to become reality very soon. He had already told James to see about changing the deed to Number Five so it was no longer in his name alone, but in both his and Mallory's. And he was going to meet with James in his Seattle office, on Monday afternoon, to sign the appropriate forms.

His plan would undoubtedly meet with stiff opposition from Mallory; James had once referred to her as being "too bloody independent," which was true. But besides being independent, she was also practical and she liked to plan ahead, so when he laid out his reasons for making the move, he was positive she would end up seeing things his way.

*   *   *

After the baby's bath, with Jordan's help Mallory dressed the infant in a white T-shirt and blue shorts, and then she slathered his exposed skin with sunscreen, and planted a floppy blue sunhat on his head.

Jordan carried him downstairs and put him in his stroller. They were just saying their goodbyes at the front door, when Jordan saw the moms come up the drive, three little ones in tow.

''When will it be safe to come back?'' he asked Mallory.

''We'll have lunch at noon.''

''Right!'' He sketched a salute. ''We'll be off then. See you later.''

The moms smiled cheerfully at him as they approached, and their children crowded around the stroller, forcing Jordan to pause.

''Hi, Matthew!'' They cooed and fussed over him—to his great delight—until the mothers said, ''Come along now, there's Mallory waiting for us at the door!''

The children ran off with their mothers and Jordan continued on his way to the street.

The sun was peeking in and out of blustery clouds, and the sea was dark gray, streaked with silver. The wind was warm but quite strong, and it riffled the brim of Matt's hat as Jordan pushed the stroller towards town.

He hadn't walked two blocks when he saw the Barnley sisters coming towards him. They took up the width of the sidewalk, so when they got closer, he rolled the stroller onto the road in order to let them pass.

But they stopped.

"Good morning, Mr. Caine." Angelina narrowed her eyes and subjected both him and Matt to a penetrating inspection. "I'm glad to see," she went on with a superior sniff, "that you are finally shouldering some of your responsibilities. Despite your previous *appalling* lapse."

"Oh, yes, Angelina!" Monique's faded blue eyes sparked with horror at the memory. "Despite that appalling lapse!"

Emily regarded the baby warmly over the top of her half glasses. "I think," she murmured, "that Matthew is a very lucky little boy, to have an uncle so devoted to him. Some men, you know, wouldn't be seen dead wheeling a baby down the street. They think it's not *macho!*"

Jordan managed to suppress a chuckle; the word had sounded odd, coming from the lips of the frail elderly woman. "You've been to town, ladies?"

"We've been to the Pink Palace for our morning coffee." Angelina's nose quivered. "It's the only place left where one can get fresh-baked scones and dairy butter."

"And homemade raspberry preserves," added Monique, with a vigorous nod.

"On our way home, we are going to pop in and see Mallory," Emily offered softly. "We've bought her a small gift—a package of gourmet coffee."

About to say, "Best not pop in just now, she already has company," Jordan bit his tongue. Mallory thrived on company. She would welcome the sisters with the same enthusiasm she'd have welcomed a Coast Guard Search and Rescue vessel if she'd been stranded on a desert island!

But as he sauntered on his way, he found himself admitting that he got a kick out of the three sisters. On first meeting them he'd thought Angelina a royal pain in the butt. Now he realized they were all genuine characters, and they were truly fond of Mallory and Matt.

While in town, he bumped into Elsa, who was obviously delighted to see him, and advised him to call in at Toldbey's, as they had Mallory's favourite chocolates on sale. "Lucky Fives," she said. "Milk chocolate, dark chocolate, nougat, marshmallow, and hazelnuts." She rolled her eyes. "In my humble opinion, they're divine!"

Dr. Scott was standing in front of the Burton Barton Realty office, talking to the realtor. They had him stop so they could say hi to Matt; then the doctor asked how Mallory's hand was coming along.

"Fine," Jordan said. "She'll be managing on her own tomorrow—I'll be leaving in the afternoon."

"But you'll be back?" Burton dabbed his perspiring brow with a yellow bandanna. "This little guy—" he nodded at Matt "—he's going to need a man in his life."

The doctor's lips twitched. "As is his aunt!"

"Mallory's footloose and fancy free." Burton's smile balled his florid cheeks. "And rumour has it, Caine, that you have a hard time keeping your eyes off the lady!''

Well, he wasn't about to deny that. Couldn't deny it, actually, because it was true.

"And she has just as hard a time keeping her eyes off you!'' said the doctor. ''I teased her about it, after Elsa's barbecue. She didn't deny it. Couldn't deny it, actually, because it was true!''

Jordan cursed silently. He did *not* want to get involved in this conversation; did not want to discuss Mallory with these two. And as Matt conveniently gave an impatient cry and started kicking his feet, he said,

"Excuse me, I'll have to get going—the baby likes to be in constant motion. See you around,'' he added smoothly.

He thought he heard them chuckling as he strode away, but his mind was already wrapped up in the doctor's words. Had Mallory really found it hard to keep her eyes off him? If so, she'd managed to do her peeking without his being aware of it. And after his uncontrolled outburst on the way home from their dinner at the Golf and Country Club, she'd been cool to him, so he'd backed off.

Given her space. Given himself some space
too…and a chance to look at the situation ob-
jectively. And when he'd done that, he'd re-
alizcd that he was becoming far too fond of
her; and he'd best reject his earlier plan to start
up a sexual liaison with her. When he left, he
didn't want there to be any emotional entan-
glement to complicate their situation.

So for the past few days he'd been casual
and friendly on the surface, and had convinced
himself that he was doing the right thing. For
both of them. It had been difficult, though.
Sometimes when he caught her off-guard, her
eyes had been sad and wistful. He'd wanted to
put his arms around her, kiss that sadness
away. But surely that would have been a mistake.…

He was mulling the matter over when he
noticed Toldbey's, and he wheeled Matt into
the store. An array of Lucky Five Chocolates
was set up on a table; he picked up a couple
of boxes and took them to the counter.

The clerk leaned over the counter and said
''Hi, there, Matthew!'' Then putting his hands
over his eyes, he said, ''Peekaboo!''

Matt hid his face with spread fingers and gurgled with delight. The clerk laughed, and after dropping the chocolate boxes in a plastic bag, said to Jordan, "These are for Mallory, right? Tell her Chance said to remember: 'A moment on the lips, a lifetime on the hips!'" He slid Jordan's change over the counter. "How's her hand? I felt real bad for her, when I heard about it. We all did."

"All?" Jordan tucked his change into his pocket.

"Everybody in town. Leastways, the ones that know her…and most do. She's a friendly one, the kind that likes people and people like her right back! She cares about folks; I guess that's what it is. And she fit right in, in our little community, from the very first."

Outside the store, Jordan bumped into Dave Matlock of Matlock's Marina; he'd been a guest at Elsa's barbecue.

"Hi," Dave said. "Don't forget my invitation to come fishing with me on Windstar. Call me, we'll set it up."

"Thanks!" Jordan said as he moved on. No point in telling Dave he wasn't going to be around after tomorrow…

But then Dave would probably know by sundown anyway. Everybody in Seashore knew what everyone else was doing—which was something he should have hated—the way he'd hated it while he was growing up in that other small town.

But, astonishingly, he didn't. It gave him a feeling of comfort, to know that Mallory was part of what was almost an extended family.

In addition, it gave him a feeling of envy, which astonished him too. The last thing he'd have expected would be that he'd ever want to become *part* of such an ''extended family.''

He'd changed in so many ways since coming to Seashore. When he'd arrived, he'd been a loner—dour and bitter and hostile. A man who didn't like redheads, didn't like babies, didn't like small towns, didn't like being around people. He shook his head disbelievingly. All that had gone by the board.

He was still mulling over this minor miracle as he took Matt to the park behind the Rec Centre, where he sat on a bench and drank a take-out coffee, while his charge sucked apple juice from the bottle Mallory had packed for him.

They stayed there till quarter to twelve, enjoying the sunshine and the warm breeze, and then they headed home.

When they got within sight of Number Five, Jordan saw a car in the drive—a top-of-the-line black Mercedes. A week ago he'd have thought, sourly, "Oh, hell, another visitor!"

Now, he just gave a rueful smile.

"Your aunt has company," he said to Matt as they walked by the vehicle. "But what else is new!" Glancing inside, he saw a neatly folded map on the dash. Somebody visiting from out of town?

Approaching the side gate leading to the backyard, he heard voices. When he pushed the gate open, he saw Mallory standing on the patio. And she was with a man.

The stranger was tall, lanky, sandy-haired. He was wearing a collarless blue shirt, navy slacks, taupe thongs.

Mallory looked flushed, and her eyes sparkled. Neither she nor her companion had heard the gate open.

But just as Jordan opened his mouth to make his presence known, the stranger reached out, grasped Mallory by the shoulders, hauled her hard against his lanky body...

And kissed her.

CHAPTER ELEVEN

GET YOUR hands off my woman!

Jordan opened his mouth to roar out the words…and then snapped it shut again, the words unsaid.

Mallory wasn't *his* woman. And it was absolutely none of his business whose hands were on her.

But the knowledge did nothing to assuage the searing jealousy burning a hole in his gut.

Even as he staggered from the unfamiliar emotion, he realized Matt had caught sight of the couple on the patio and the child had no qualms about roaring *his* disapproval!

Startled by the baby's indignant cry, Mallory wrenched herself from her companion, and with a loud gasp, shoved him back. The stranger lost his balance and staggered sideways, coming up against the picnic table. Collapsing on the bench with a thump, he fixed confused hazel eyes on Jordan.

Mallory's brown eyes were also fixed on Jordan…but hers weren't confused. They were *furious*. As was her voice, when she cried, "Where have you *been!*"

He blinked…and felt as confused as her visitor. "We were at the park—you said lunch wouldn't be till noon—"

She threw up her hands and spinning around so fast her auburn hair spread out like an explosion of flame, she stormed into the house and slammed the door behind her.

Jordan gawked after her. What the hell had got into *her?* Was she suffering from P.M.S.…or was she just furious that he'd interrupted the sizzling kiss she'd been sharing with the owner of the brand-new black Mercedes?

At any rate, the little melodrama had diverted Matt and defused his outrage. Chewing a tiny fist with his gums, he watched unblinkingly as the stranger got up from the bench, and hand outstretched, walked over to join them.

"I'm Nick Sullivan," he said. "You must be Jordan Caine."

"Nick Sullivan?" Jordan echoed, as they shook hands. Where had he heard that name before?

"Mallory's fiancé."

Wham! That was where he'd heard it before. Of course.

"I thought you two had broken up." He tried to keep his hostility from showing. "Mallory said—"

"We did have a slight disagreement." Nick used pale fingers to sweep back his overly long brown hair. "But the situation has changed. We're back on track." He tossed an uninterested glance at Matt. "This is the kid?"

The *kid?* Jordan's hackles rose. What way was that to refer to this adorable little—

Uh-oh. Wait up. Wasn't that exactly how he himself had referred to Matt, before he'd got to know him? Oh, boy, had he *ever* come a long way—

"Well, is it or isn't it?" Nick's tone was careless.

"Yes," Jordan said, and added pointedly, "this is the *baby.* Our nephew. Mallory's and mine."

But Nick was looking at his watch. "I've got to be going." His attention was already elsewhere.

"This is only a flying visit?" Jordan felt a spark of hope.

"Yeah. Just had to drive here from Seattle to tell Mallory something, not the kind of news you want to give over the phone..." He looked at the house. "Is she going to come out again...?"

"News?" Jordan pressed.

"Good news. The best. Got word from my agent, late last night—my new book, the one I've been working on for the past couple of years—my publisher's offered a two-million-dollar advance. I knew Mallory would be ecstatic—not that she cares about money, but it means our problems are over. The thing that came between us—the matter of the kid—now we can afford a bigger place, and a full-time nanny to keep him out of my hair..."

Jordan felt as if someone had run an ice cube down his spine. Nobody, but *nobody* was going to hire a nanny to look after his nephew—

Hey, wait up—again! Before he'd got to know Mallory, hadn't he himself planned to use *her* for that very purpose? His mind boggled at the distance he'd come in a few days—

"And in the event I can't get her to agree to that," Nick continued, "we'll have to make sure the new place will be big enough that he can be kept out of earshot. Did you *hear* him bellow just now? No way can I write with that kind of a din going on. Come to think of it, I wonder if it's possible to find a house *big* enough to get away from his racket—maybe we need to be thinking 'soundproof room'!"

"For you?"

"For the kid." Nick glanced restlessly at his watch again. "I'm going inside. I have to talk to Mallory. D'you mind giving us some time?"

Mind? Of course he damn well minded! "Go ahead," he said. "I'll take Matt down to the beach…"

But the wildly successful author and owner of a brand-spanking-new Mercedes had already opened the back door.

Jordan scooped Matt out of his stroller. "C'mon, little tyke." He planted a tender kiss on the baby's brow. "Let's get out of here before I wring that guy's scrawny white neck."

Mallory watched from her bedroom window as Jordan scooped up the baby and gave him a tender kiss. The sight made her want to weep.

She sighed, and laid her brow against the windowpane. Imagine Nick turning up like that. After the finality of their parting, it was the last thing she'd expected.

Then when he'd told her his news, she'd been stunned. And while she was standing there, trying to gather enough breath to congratulate him on his fantastic breakthrough, he'd announced they could get back together now. And before she'd recovered from the shock of his arrogance, he'd hauled her into his arms and given her a resounding kiss.

At which moment, of course, Jordan had come home— And she had, unfairly, vented all her outrage and frustration on him. If only he'd arrived ten minutes earlier, he'd have been there to act as a buffer...

Oh, who are you kidding! she thought. What had really made her so angry was that it was *Nick* who had hauled her into his arms and overpowered her with his kiss, when *Jordan* was the one she wanted—

''Mallory?'' Nick's voice drifted from downstairs. ''Darling?''

She saw that Jordan had walked across the street and was headed for the beach, with Matt on his shoulders. The sight brought an ache to her heart. An ache of longing.

Why, she thought despairingly, could things not have been different?

Brushing away a tear, she sent a last yearning look after Jordan and the baby, and then made her way downstairs.

When Jordan returned to the house, the Mercedes was gone.

Mallory was in the kitchen and he could see she'd been crying. So despite his gnawing need to ask questions, he decided he'd leave her to talk about Nick when she was ready. He gave her the Lucky Fives, hoping to cheer her up, but her smile and her murmur of thanks were distracted.

She didn't speak much during lunch, and afterwards, when she took Matt upstairs to put him down for his nap, Jordan wandered through to the sitting room. He prowled around abstractedly, ending up at a rattan bookcase.

He picked out a Dick Francis paperback, and when he flipped it open, he saw that the novel had belonged to Tom. The inscription on the flyleaf read: To my brother the Fish, on his twenty-fourth birthday. All my love, Mallory.

He compressed his lips as he recalled overhearing Tom's best man remark to someone, during the wedding reception, that he'd thrown a party on the occasion of Tom's twenty-fourth birthday, and it was there that Tom and Janine had first met.

As he thought about Tom, Jordan's anger and resentment at Mallory's brother flared to life again—and he didn't try to extinguish it. He knew better. The bitter feeling would always be with him; would always rankle…

He rammed the book back onto the shelf but he knocked another book over and it fell to the floor. He put it back. But Mallory must have been on her way downstairs and heard the clatter because a moment later she came into the room.

"Hi," she murmured.

He turned, and felt a surge of concern when he saw dry tear tracks on her flushed cheeks. Damn that man for making her cry! "Hi," he said. "Matt asleep?"

She nodded. "He's dozing off." She hesitated, and then said quietly, "I expect you want to talk."

"Only if you feel up to it."

Crossing to the window seat, she sat in one corner, against the wall, and tucked her legs under her.

"I've been so blind," she said, looking at him. "All those years I spent with Nick, I never realized how self-centered he is. I guess I made excuses for him—I know that writers get tremendously involved in their work, but it's more than that with him. He's not interested in anyone or anything but himself...he doesn't have any...compassion."

"What happened?" Jordan asked as he came to stand over her. "After I took Matt down to the beach?"

"He wanted me to take back the ring he'd given me—I didn't want it." Her voice shook. "He couldn't seem to understand that I didn't want him either."

She didn't want Nick Sullivan. Jordan felt giddy with relief.

"He thought," Mallory went on, "that because he'll have all that money, things would be perfect. They would've been—" her smile was wry "—for *him*. But not for me. Anyway, I told him you and I had a deal—a contract— so even if I'd wanted to marry him, I couldn't have."

Jordan frowned. "Mallory—" he sat on the window seat, facing her, his eyes grave "—I'd never hold you to that. Not now. We've got to know each other the past week and a half and I trust you completely. I trust you enough to know that if you ever *did* decide to marry, it would only be to a man who loved Matt. I'd never stand in the way of your happiness. It's important to me. *You* are important to me."

She thought how important he had become to her too. And how very dear. In fact, she was so besotted with him she could have whiled away the rest of her life just looking at his face—adoring those heavily-lashed gray eyes, that slightly off-kilter nose, that sensually full lower lip...

"Mallory?"

She dragged her gaze up from his oh-so-tempting mouth. "Thank you, Jordan. But I won't marry. No man could *ever* love Matt as much as I'd need him to."

He took her left hand in his, and careful not to hurt it, he turned the hand over. Tracing a fingertip over her bare ring finger, he said, "*I do.*"

The intensity of his tone made her nervous. To cover up, she said lightly, "Yes...but you're not a marrying man!"

"We had a conversation like this—it seems eons ago—when we were discussing our four options. At that time, I suggested we get married—a marriage of convenience. You refused me point-blank. But things are different now—"

"Jordan, I don't want to discuss this—"

"Hear me out. As I said, things are different now. We know each other. And we like each other—" He raised his eyebrows. "You do like me, don't you?"

Like him? She'd have walked around the world barefoot for him. "Yes, I like you." She kept her tone as casual as if he'd asked whether she liked her coffee black.

"We could have a great marriage." His eyes had taken on a burning expression that made her shiver inside. "We both love Matt and he'd bind us together. He's almost like our own child, what with the blood ties...your brother and my sister being his parents. I believe marriage would turn out to be the very best thing. Maybe the stumbling block, last time around, was that neither of us trusted the other."

She lowered her gaze, unable to meet his eyes as she thought of the shattering truth she was keeping from him. If only she could bare her soul, tell him that Tom wasn't Matt's father. But she was honor-bound to keep that secret and no way could she marry Jordan while it lay like a black chasm between them. A chasm he didn't know existed, but a chasm that would forever block her from the happiness beckoning from the other side.

He tipped her chin up with a fingertip. "You do trust me, don't you?"

At least she needn't lie about that. "Yes."

Puzzlement flickered across his face. "Then why won't you—"

"I can't."

He frowned. "Is there something I don't know?"

"Yes." She forced the word out. "But it's not something I can talk about."

"You're not making sense. You say you trust me but you're keeping secrets from me. Mallory—"

"You say you trust me too…and you'll have to trust me on this. I'm sorry, Jordan. That's the end of it." She paused a moment to steady herself, and then went on, in an unnaturally bright tone, "While you were out, James brought over our paperwork. If we okay it, we're to sign it and—"

Jordan shot up from his seat. He shoved his hands in his hip pockets and glared down at her. "It's not enough for me, Mallory." His eyes glittered with exasperation—and something else. Something that fluttered her heart and set her pulsebeat off in a wild race. "Dammit, woman," he growled, "I'm not proposing a marriage of convenience this time, I'm proposing a real marriage. And not because I want security for Matt but because I've fallen in love with you!''

He hadn't meant to say it. Hadn't even known he was going to say it! The words had emerged from his mouth before they'd even formed in his brain. But they were the right words, and as soon as they were out there, he'd felt giddy with joy. He'd fallen in love with this woman, and how he hadn't realized it before, he hadn't the foggiest idea.

And he might never have realized it, if he hadn't experienced that agonizing jealousy at seeing her in another man's arms.

But she was having none of it. Having none of him.

As his proposal had echoed around the room, she'd stared at him with eyes that had gone from startled to stunned to stark in five beats of his heart.

''No.'' She'd whispered the rejection. ''I can't.''

Stumbling to her feet, she'd fled from the room.

*　　*　　*

Mallory stayed upstairs till Matt woke from his nap. She spent most of that time curled up on her bed, crying. Crying because Jordan had fallen in love with her; crying because she couldn't have him. She spent the rest of the time applying a cold damp facecloth to her eyes and cheeks, in an attempt to clear the evidence of her weeping.

But she needn't have worried about Jordan's seeing her blotched face or her red swollen eyelids, because when she brought Matt downstairs, she found that he'd gone out.

He'd left a note on the kitchen table. GONE FOR A HIKE. DON'T MAKE DINNER FOR ME. Beside the note was James's contract.

Jordan had signed it.

Her depression deepened even further. So...he'd accepted her rejection and was returning to their original plan. She should have felt relieved—relieved that he wasn't going to hang around and put more pressure on her. Instead, she felt as if her life had become empty.

And that was bewildering, because she had Matt; wriggly little Matt who at this very moment, even as she gazed despairingly at

Jordan's strong black signature, was trying to pull a lock of her auburn hair into his mouth!

She hugged him close, and kissed him, before setting him into his high chair for his afternoon snack.

''I love you,'' she whispered. And wished with all her heart that she could have said those words to his uncle.

That night, Jordan's nightmare came again.

He awoke drenched in sweat, and shaking.

Cursing savagely under his breath, he threw back his sheet, and got out of bed. He crossed to the open window, and stood there, letting the breeze cool his fevered body.

It had been the worst episode yet. Strapped to the tree trunk, blindfolded, he'd heard the click of the gun not once but over and over again, and each time he died—

''Jordan?''

Inhaling a shuddering breath, he turned and saw Mallory walking across the shadowy room. In the thin light from the moon, he saw that her face was white, her eyes dark with worry. She had a glass in her hand. And she held it out.

He walked to meet her and took the drink. He'd expected water; what he got was Scotch.

"I'm sorry," he said.

She slid her hands into the pockets of her robe. "For what?"

"For wakening you." He took a gulp from the glass and then another.

"The nightmare again."

"Thankfully it doesn't happen often."

"It's the fourth time," she said gently, "since you've been here."

Damn. "Then I must apologize again."

"Why should you? It's not as if you have any control over them."

"That's true. But still…" He finished the Scotch, but when she made to take the glass from him, he set it on the bedside table and caught her wrist. "Don't go."

He sensed her hesitation, and then she said, in a low voice, "I'll stay—but only if you'll talk to me."

"About what?"

"About…where you think these bad dreams are coming from."

"Hell," he said roughly, "I know where they're coming from!"

"You said you'd had some bad experiences—in Zlobovia?"

He didn't respond.

"Were they…connected in some way with that woman, the one who was married with two—"

"I don't want to talk about it."

"But you must! Don't you see that? The longer you keep it all bottled inside, the more disturbing your nightmares are going to be!"

She was right. He knew it. But talking about it meant reliving the memories. The prospect alone caused adrenaline to surge through him, churning his gut.

He dropped her wrist and wheeling around, strode back to the window. Pressing his hands to the side frames, he tried to steady his erratic heartbeat. Tried to relax the muscles clenching his stomach.

"Jordan." She had come up behind him. "Talk to me."

His gaze blurred as he stared out unseeingly over the starlit ocean.

"Please!"

The anguish in her tone demolished his defences the way nothing else could. He took several deep breaths. Long slow breaths, in an attempt to calm himself. Then he said, finally and in a low voice, ''The woman's name is Zoe Brokaw. Her husband's a mine owner. I was contracted by his company to drill at a site in Zlobovia, right in the middle of rebel country. Brokaw went missing—the day I was to fly home for Janine's funeral. He'd been kidnapped by guerillas and taken to their camp upriver. Zoe came to me for help.''

''Oh, Jordan!'' Her voice cracked. ''I wish you could have told me! But I realize now that it was too difficult for you to talk about it. But...why did Zoe come to you? Why not to...to the authorities?''

His laugh was ironic. ''Honey, where we were, there *were* no authorities.''

''When we talked about this before, you said you left with the woman because she wanted your services...and I misunderstood. But you also said she knew what kind of a man you were...and now I realize that what you meant by that was, she knew you were the kind of man she could rely on to get a job done. But still,'' she bit her lip, ''it must have been a hard choice to make, since it meant missing

Janine's funeral. I know how dearly you loved your sister.''

"I had no choice. Remember Fred, the old guy who gave me my start, up in Alaska? Fred saved my life not long after I arrived up there—a grizzly came at me, he shot it. I owed him. And I owed him for my biggest contracts too, because it was through him that I met Brokaw. Brokaw and his wife used to visit Fred from time to time, and I got to know them.'' He turned and looked down at her. "Zoe Brokaw was Fred's daughter.''

Mallory gave a little gasp. "Oh, I see. So...when she came to you for help, you couldn't possibly have refused.'' She paused for a moment, then she said, "Did you *find* him?''

"I found him. And luck was on my side— I managed to get him out of there. We lost each other shortly after leaving the camp...and that's when Lady Luck deserted me. The guerillas caught up with me and took me to a camp—a different one, deep in the mountains. Nobody could ever have found it.'' He felt sick as the memories of that time pressed to the forefront of his mind. "Although I found out later that Brokaw spared no effort in his attempts to do so. Anyway, I was there for eight months, before I managed to escape. And that time, Lady Luck was with me.''

For a long moment, the room was silent. Then Mallory said, in a low voice, ''And the nightmares...they're from what happened to you during those eight months?''

''Let's just say the rebels were not amused by what I'd done. They'd intended holding Brokaw for ransom and I'd done them out of that money. In my own case, before I set out to look for him, I'd got rid of all my ID and made it clear to Zoe that I would only go after her husband on the condition that if I too went missing, there was to be a cover-up. Nobody, but nobody, was to know. I was bound and determined that no ransom be paid for my release if I were captured. So when I *was* taken, the rebels didn't know who I was and couldn't find out...but they held me accountable for denying them Brokaw's ransom money. They made me pay.'' His lips tightened. ''In other ways.''

''Torture?''

"Mental torture. Their particular brand of Russian roulette."

"Oh, Jordan…"

"Sweetheart, don't cry." But the words came too late, he could see her face twist, her eyes fill with tears. He put his arms around and held her close. "It's over," he murmured, stroking her hair, "and you were right, I feel better now I've talked about it." He ran his fingers through the loose curls. "I never thought I'd be able to, but with you…"

"I'm glad." Her voice was muffled against his chest. "But I can't bear the idea of you going through all that—"

"Hey!" He tried to lighten the moment. "I'm macho! At least, that's what Emily called me when she saw me wheel the stroller along the street—"

Mallory made a sound between a sob and a chuckle. "Oh, Emily," she whispered with a catch in her voice. "She's a funny one—she's never been married but she does know a thing or two about men." She looked up at him. "She really likes you, Jordan."

"And how do *you* feel about me?"

She bit her lip. "Jordan, don't—"

"You know how I feel about you, Mallory. I've fallen in love with you. I told you that. What I don't know, because I didn't ask, was...are my feelings returned?"

She averted her face but he framed it between his hands and made her look at him again.

"I'm not the kind of guy," he said softly, "that makes a pest of himself. I'm not the kind of guy who pushes himself at a woman who doesn't want him. And I won't bring this up again if you can look me in the eye and say you don't want me. Can you?" he asked. "Can you do that?"

He could sense the struggle going on inside her. She didn't want to admit the truth; but she had too much integrity to lie.

"No," she said at last. "I can't deny the attraction between us—the *sexual* attraction—"

"Oh, there's so much more." He couldn't keep the urgency from his tone. "More than just that basic chemistry, that sexual connection. I'm talking about an emotional connection. We're kindred spirits, Mallory. Twin souls. Meant for each other. I *know* you must feel it, it's too powerful to be one-sided. Can you look me in the eye and swear you don't feel that connection too?''

''No,'' she whispered. ''I can't, but—''

He claimed her lips in a kiss that drowned out any ''buts.'' A kiss that made him weak at the knees; a kiss that made her tremble as she arched up against him with a moan.

The little sound drove his desire to new heights. Frantic for her, he swung her around and pressed her against the wall, feeling the thrust of her breasts against his naked chest. Deepening the kiss, he was almost overcome by the hot sweet taste of her; the amber Oriental scent from her warm body. With a groan, he slid his hands between them, opened her robe, slipped it over her shoulders and let it fall to the floor.

And all the time, they kissed. Kissed with open mouths, wet and soft, then his tongue was sliding against hers, hers was coiling around his, erotically, uninhibitedly, desperately. Blindly he found the spaghetti straps of her nightie; worked them down, till the silky garment slithered to join her robe on the floor.

She dug her hands into his hair and clutched it, whimpering with need, and he swept her up in his arms and carried her to the bed. In a second she was lying on her back, and he was over her, supporting himself with his hands spread out on the mattress, either side of her head. Her body was pale, her hair a slash of fire.

He held himself taut above her, holding himself back. Before they made love—and he knew they were going to make love, knew it by the passion clouding her brown eyes, the restless way she clung to his shoulders—before he made love to her, he wanted to tell her how happy she had made him.

"Sweetheart," he whispered, "I knew you loved me. Just as much as I love you. Whatever it was that held you back, it doesn't matter. I don't care *what* your secret is! All that matters now is that we're together...and I'll never let you down. When we get married—"

Her hands tightened on his shoulders. She blinked, as if his words had drawn her from some far place. "Jordan," her voice shook, "I won't marry you. I've told you that."

He stared at her incredulously. "You would make love with me…but you won't marry me?"

She closed her eyes.

It was all the answer he needed.

He could have had her, if he wanted. She was his for the taking. And for a fraction of a second, he was tempted. Tempted just as Adam had been by Eve, in the Garden of Eden.

But he wanted more from this woman than just sex.

He pushed himself off the bed and as he stood at the bedside, she looked up at him with tear-starred eyes.

"Sex is not enough." His voice was hard. Implacable. "I want it all. I want your love, and I want your hand in marriage. Unless you can offer me that, we have nothing."

CHAPTER TWELVE

JORDAN LEFT early next morning.

With Matt in her arms, Mallory walked to the end of the drive and watched his Lexus disappear along the street. She'd managed to keep her tears in check as she and Jordan said their goodbyes; now they welled up as she recalled the conversation they'd had just before he got in the car.

"I've given James instructions," he told her, "to have the house put in both our names, joint tenancy."

Dismayed, she'd said, "I don't *want* you to—"

He'd waved aside her protest. "It's in Matt's best interests. In the event that anything should happen to me, the house will automatically become yours. It'll save a lot of hassle and it'll ensure that you and Matt will always have a home. There'll be nothing to stop you putting the house in his name, if you want to, when he's old enough."

How could she argue with his reasoning? She couldn't. And she didn't. Like Jordan, she had Matt's best interests at heart, and the plan was a practical one. But she was absolutely staggered that despite his knowing she was keeping something from him, he trusted her so completely.

"You'll have papers to sign," he went on. "But James will see to everything." His gray gaze was without emotion. "Do you have any problem with this arrangement?"

She shook her head. "No. It's...a sensible plan." As he turned his attention to the baby, she couldn't stop herself from blurting out the question burning on her lips: "When will you be back?"

"Oh, someday." He ruffled Matt's hair casually but when the baby responded with a joyous "Da...da!" his face tightened and her heart went out to him. She knew what a wrench it must be, leaving his little nephew.

"You'll...be in touch?" she said.

He turned away, and opened his car door. "I'll send a postcard, now and again. Just to let you know I'm alive."

"Thank you," she said. "And good luck with your contact in Australia." She wanted to keep him, just a little while longer. "What's the man's name?"

"Jerry Stanton."

"I hope all goes well."

"I hope so too."

Then he got in the car and drove away. Without kissing her. Without even touching her. And without so much as a backward glance.

"I'm afraid Mr. Stanton's in a meeting." The Stanton Mining Company's receptionist, a willowy blonde, displayed her pearly whites to Jordan in a seductive smile that sent the clear message that *she* was available! Gesturing towards the waiting area, she said, "Can I get you…anything?"

"No, thanks." He found her boldness a turn-off—though he had to admit that just a month ago, he'd probably have flirted in response to her blatant come-on.

Now, she left him cold. As would every other female.

It was, of course, Mallory's fault. Taking a seat, he picked up a magazine and started flipping the pages. Dammit, that woman had ruined him for anyone else—

He stopped flipping as something caught his eye in an article on the signs of the Zodiac. He'd never gone in for horoscopes and suchlike…but he frowned at the words that had jumped out at him: Pisces. The Fish.

To my brother the Fish. That had been Mallory's inscription on the flyleaf of Tom's Dick Francis novel. At the time, he hadn't spared a second to wonder what it meant.

Now he knew.

Because he had nothing better to do, he checked to see what his own sign was. His birthday lay between March 20 and April 20, so it appeared he was an Aries. Aries, the Ram. And his personality type was: Leader.

Moving his gaze down the page, he checked for the personality type of the Pisces—birthdate between February 19 and March 20—and saw that it specified: Communicator.

It also specified that the Pisces was a strategist.

Huh! What strategy had Tom the Fish used, he wondered bitterly, to get Janine into his bed!

Feeling suddenly jet-lagged and jaded, he flung the magazine down and sprawling back, closed his eyes.

It was no good dwelling on the past, he told himself. Snap out of it! But though he tried to focus his mind on the upcoming meeting with Stanton, he couldn't stop thinking about what he'd just read in the magazine.

Something niggled at him. He didn't know what it was, but it wouldn't let go. Something didn't fit. And his subconscious knew it even though his conscious mind didn't.

What the *hell* was it!

He jerked himself up from his sprawling position and reached for the magazine again.

He read everything he'd read before. Read it and reread it. And then read it again. He was scouring it for what must have been the tenth time, when he heard Stanton's office door opening.

The sound tugged at him...but the horoscope page tugged at him more. Over the mur-

mur of men's voices, he vaguely heard the secretary say, "Goodbye, gentlemen!"

With the magazine still in his hand, his eyes
still on the page, he got to his feet.

"Mr. Caine," the secretary called over,
"Mr. Stanton will see you now."

"Yeah," he said abstractedly. "Be right
there—"

His gaze kept returning to the line that read:

*Pisces. Birthdate between February 19 and
March 20.*

He sensed that the answer was there. But
what was the import of those dates? It took
him a couple more minutes to figure it out—
and when he finally understood the implication, he felt as shocked and benumbed as if
he'd been plunged headfirst and stark naked
into a glacial lake.

Dear God. The magazine shook in his grasp.
His head became dizzy. Did this *really* mean
what it seemed to mean?

If it did, it changed everything.
Everything.

"Mr. Caine." The receptionist's voice was
impatient. "I said, Mr. Stanton will see you
now."

He blinked and glanced up.

The blonde frowned at him. "Is there something wrong? You look as if you've just seen a ghost!"

Oh, yes, he thought with a sick-to-his-stomach feeling. If his suspicions turned out to be fact, then for the rest of his life he *would* be seeing a ghost.

Tom's ghost.

"I'm fine." Gathering himself together with an effort, he dropped the magazine on the table and headed towards the open doorway of Stanton's office. "But while I'm in with your boss, could you call me a cab and have it waiting." He rubbed a hand over his nape and his fingers came away slick with sweat. "I need to get to the airport."

Feeling unbearably restless and depressed the weekend after Jordan left, Mallory decided to throw a potluck supper on the Saturday evening. Everybody she invited was able to come; and everybody studiously avoided talking about Jordan.

Except Meg.

After dinner, while they were sitting alone on the patio, Meg said, quietly,

"Have you heard anything from Jordan?"

"No." Mallory used a bright tone to hide her sadness. "And I don't expect to, not for a while."

"You're missing him, though. You must be."

"I'm lucky to have my friends," Mallory said, not responding directly to Meg's comment. And as she looked around the yard, she knew that she was, indeed, lucky, to have friends she could count on.

Elsa was standing at the swing set, pushing Matt gently on the smallest swing. The sisters were strolling by the flowerbeds, commenting with delight on each tender bud. Sam and Dave Matlock were in the far corner, digging a vegetable patch for her. Tyler strolled from group to group, wineglass in hand, the picture of elegance in a sleek navy sweater and immaculately pressed taupe slacks. Dee and James were up for the weekend and Mallory could hear them chatting in the kitchen as they washed the dinner dishes.

"Isn't it wonderful," she said in an attempt to change the subject, "that Dee's pregnant! I was so happy to hear her news today."

"Mmm. Me too! It's going to be fun having two babies in the family! And speaking of babies...how are the plans for your day care coming along?"

"Oh, I'm not in any rush. I've decided not to start up till September, when the schools go in."

"You don't seem as enthusiastic about the project as you were in the beginning."

Mallory stifled a sigh. Meg was right. She just couldn't work up any interest in it. Couldn't work up any interest in anything. Not even in the house—and she knew the reason for that. Without Jordan, Number Five no longer felt like home. Home for her was wherever *he* was. If things had been different, she'd have followed him to the ends of the earth and made her home wherever he hung his hat.

Only he never wore a hat. And even if he did, he wouldn't hang it here. Not when she wouldn't commit to him. Not when she wouldn't marry him.

And she never could.

This time, her sigh came from her soul and she was unable to suppress it.

"Oh, sweetie." Meg reached over and patted her arm. "I'm sorry. I shouldn't have talked about Jordan. Elsa warned me not to. But I can't believe I was wrong. I so believed that the two of you were meant for each other."

Mallory got up from her chair as tears sprang to her eyes. "It's all right, Meg." She felt a sob rising. "Will you excuse me, just for a minute?"

Without waiting for an answer, she fled into the house, hurrying past James and Dee in the kitchen without a word.

She ran upstairs, went into the bathroom, and locked the door. Sitting on the edge of the bath, she put her head on her hands and gave in to the tears that welled up from her heart, tears of anguished longing for the man she couldn't have.

The sun was setting when Jordan left the highway and drove along Seaside Lane towards Number Five. The sky was a riot of pink and gold, the surface of the ocean smooth as cream and painted with streaks of rose and lavender, the sight so poignantly beautiful it made his heart ache.

The evening was warm, and he could smell the salt-tang of the sea, hear the rhythmic murmur of the waves, along with the cry of a wheeling gull. The anticipation that had been building inside him since his plane landed now reached a crescendo. He couldn't wait to see Mallory.

He only hoped that when he got there, she'd be alone.

But when he came within sight of the house, his hopes were dashed. Three vehicles were crammed into her short drive: Sam's black Infiniti, a van with the Matlock Marina logo, and Tyler Scott's flashy white Jag.

But as he parked his Lexus in the street, despite himself he had to smile. Mallory loved company; it seemed some things never changed.

When Mallory came downstairs again, it was with a feeling of defeat. Her face was a blotchy mess and they'd all know she'd been crying.

But they were her friends. They would understand.

She walked across the front hall and went through to the kitchen. Dee and James had finished up and the room was neat as a pin. But to her surprise, when she went outside, there was nobody in the yard. And as she looked over the fence, she saw that there were no vehicles in the drive.

Apparently everyone had gone home.

But where was Matt? Had Elsa put him to bed?

She went back inside and through the kitchen, but as she crossed the front hall, she stopped short. And froze.

On the rack, by the door, hung a hat.

A crisp new hat.

A gray felt hat.

An Aussie hat.

An Akubra.

She stared at it, suddenly finding breathing difficult. Then at last making herself move, she walked unsteadily across to the rack, and was about to lift the Akubra from its hook when she heard a sound behind her.

She spun around, and at sight of Jordan she felt her heart stand still. Felt time stand still—something she'd believed happened only in fiction. In make-believe. But this wasn't make-believe.

Jordan was real. Disheveled, stubble-bearded, and exhausted-looking, but real. And more heartbreakingly attractive than possible, even in his rumpled shirt and travel-worn khaki chinos.

Dazed—and bedazzled—she pressed a hand to her breastbone and struggled to keep her wobbling knees from giving way under her.

At last she found her voice. ''Where...why...?'' she stumbled over the words.

''I know,'' he said softly. ''I know everything.''

He could tell she'd been crying. Her eyes were red-rimmed and swollen, her face was flushed...but now he saw the colour drain slowly from her cheeks.

''Know...what?'' She spoke chokingly.

''I know that Tom couldn't have been Matt's father.''

She stared at him, her expression blank with shock. She'd become so still she could have been frozen. A statue. Then he saw her throat move as she swallowed hard. "But…" She swallowed again. "You…can't!"

"Are you *denying* it?"

She clasped her arms around herself. "What makes you think…?"

"I don't *think,* Mallory. I *know*."

The finality of his tone must have convinced her. He had never seen anyone look so shattered.

"But how…? How did I slip up?" She shook her head, as if trying to clear it. "How did I give it away?"

"You didn't."

"Then…it was nothing I said?" Her voice shook, he saw relief flood into her eyes. "Oh, I hope so, because I *promised* Janine I'd never tell…"

"It was nothing you said. Trust me."

She swayed and he thought she was going to keel over.

"Oh, dammit," he growled, moving fast to close the space between them, "I'm doing this all wrong."

He took her in his arms and pulled her close as her legs sagged. She seemed thinner and more fragile than he remembered, and he felt overcome by love, overwhelmed by regret. He'd caused her so much pain by deserting her when she wouldn't accept his marriage proposal; when—for reasons then unknown to him—she felt she *couldn't* accept it. But he'd make it up to her, in every way he possibly could.

"Sweetheart," he caressed away a tear from her eyelashes, "I found out purely by chance. I knew from something his best man said that Tom and Janine had met on Tom's twenty-fourth birthday. And I gathered, from an inscription you'd written in one of his books, that his Zodiac sign was Pisces." He told her about the magazine in the mining company's head office. "Now I already knew that Matt was a full-term baby, born in August...and when I put all the dates together, I knew that Tom couldn't possibly have been the father."

"Janine made me *promise* never to tell you. So I couldn't. Ever."

"Which leaves me with one question—"

"You want to know the identity of Matthew's father."

"Yeah," he said tautly. "If not Tom, then...who?"

"I don't know his name but he's a lecturer at one of the community colleges in Seattle— in his midforties and married. Janine met him when she was checking out courses. He took advantage of her, seduced her...and then dumped her. That was when she found out he wasn't separated from his wife, as he'd told her; he was still well and truly married. It wasn't till later that she found out she was pregnant. She never told him...he'd made it clear when he dumped her that he wanted nothing more to do with her."

Jordan spat out a word that gave vent to his feelings. And immediately apologized for swearing.

"Don't worry," Mallory said with a sigh. "I feel exactly the same about him."

"Why the hell didn't Janine tell me!"

"She was afraid you'd think badly of her. Afraid you'd think her...like your father."

He muttered frustratedly. "She should have known better," he said. "She was nothing like him. She was just young and immature and foolish.'' He took in a deep breath. ''Where did Tom come into the picture?''

''Earlier on the day of his birthday party, she'd found out she was pregnant. She was terrified. Tom found her crying in a corner, and they talked. At first, he just felt sorry for her, wanted to comfort her. They started seeing each other, and before long—well it was like magic—they fell head over heels in love. Tom proposed—and he was happy to take on Janine's baby and let people believe it was his.''

Jordan felt shame and remorse deep in his gut. ''It's too late now,'' he said. ''But…how I wish I could turn the clock back. I was so wrong about your brother.''

''He didn't hold it against you, Jordan. He told me that if he'd been in your shoes, he'd have acted the same way you did. He was sure that if you knew the truth you'd feel differently.''

''Yet he went along with Janine's desire for secrecy—and had to endure my contempt—wholly undeserved contempt!—as a result.''

''He loved her.''

Jordan took her shoulders and held her back a little so he could look into her eyes. ''And you wouldn't marry me, because you felt you would have been living a lie.''

''I hated having it between us. And in the beginning, before I got to know what kind of man you were, I was terrified you'd find out because I believed you'd take the baby away from me if you knew he wasn't Tom's.''

''Blood ties. Family ties.'' He groaned. ''If I used those terms once, I must have used them ten times. They seemed so important to me. The only thing that's important to me now is that the three of us are together.'' He wove his hands through her glorious hair, and excitement throbbed through him as he took her lips in a hot sweet kiss. A kiss that she returned with a passion that made them both breathless. When at last, he drew his mouth from hers, she whispered, against his jaw,

''When do you have to go back to Australia?''

He nuzzled her neck. ''Stanton offered me the contract but I told him that I had matters to attend to. Things to do. I told him,'' he paused to nibble the dainty lobe of her ear, ''that I was planning to take me a wife.''

Mallory arched her head back and looked at him with a teasing twinkle in her eyes. ''So...you finally decided to hang up your hat!''

''This is home,'' he said simply.

She ran tender fingertips over his jaw. ''And you think your new wife would expect you to *stay* there?''

He raised his eyebrows. ''Doesn't she?''

''The place she calls home, Jordan, is wherever *she* hangs your hat!'' She swept his Akubra from the rack and planted it firmly on his head. ''The place she calls home is wherever her husband's work takes him. And it seems as if for the next year...or more,'' she slipped her arms around his neck, ''that home is going to be Down Under!''

His delighted grin made her heart sing.

''And what about Matt?'' he asked. ''How will he feel?''

She laughed, and her dimple twinkled. ''He'll feel exactly the same way. But speaking of Matt, where *is* he?''

"I put him to bed…after I ordered everyone to leave."

"You *ordered* my guests to leave? Bossy, bossy!"

"I'm not prepared to have an audience," he said huskily, "for what I plan to do with you tonight."

She blushed. "And what would that be, Mr. Caine?"

With a melodramatic flourish, he transferred the Akubra from his head to hers, setting it rakishly in place. Then sweeping her off her feet, he strode towards the stairs.

"Hang on, Scarlett. You're about to find out!"